HAVE A HIGHLAND FLING WITH
M. C. BEATON'S

HAMISH MACBETH MYSTERIES

"This series is pure bliss."

—*Atlanta Journal-Constitution*

"The detective novels of M. C. Beaton, a master of outrageous black comedy...have reached cult status in the United States."

—*The Times Magazine* (London)

"An intimate look at life in a small Scottish village, striking insights into human nature, carefully detailed, highly accurate descriptions of police work, splendid dry humor...as pleasantly satisfying as a cozy cup of tea."

—*Booklist*

"Macbeth is the sort of character who slyly grows on you...as you realize that beneath his unassuming exterior, he's a whiz at cutting through all the hokum."

—*Chicago Sun-Times*

Death *of a* Snob

More Hamish Macbeth Mysteries by M. C. Beaton

M.C. BEATON

Death of a Snob

GRAND CENTRAL
PUBLISHING

NEW YORK   BOSTON

This book is a work of fiction. Names, characters, places, and incidents are the product of the author's imagination or are used fictitiously. Any resemblance to actual events, locales, or persons, living or dead, is coincidental.

Grand Central Publishing
Hachette Book Group
1290 Avenue of the Americas
New York, NY 10104
www.HachetteBookGroup.com

Grand Central Publishing is a division of Hachette Book Group, Inc. The Grand Central Publishing name and logo is a trademark of Hachette Book Group, Inc.

The Hachette Speakers Bureau provides a wide range of authors for speaking events. To find out more, go to www.hachettespeakersbureau.com or call (866) 376-6591.

The publisher is not responsible for websites (or their content) that are not owned by the publisher.

Printed in the United States of America

First Grand Central Publishing mass market edition: August 2013

10 9 8 7

OPM

For Jim and Barbara Hendry
of Golspie, Sutherland

Death *of a* Snob

Chapter One

Heap on more wood!—the wind is chill;
But let it whistle as it will,
We'll keep our Christmas merry still.

—Sir Walter Scott

Police constable Hamish Macbeth was a desperate man—ill, friendless, and, at the approach to Christmas, near to death.

Or so he told himself.

The start of the misery had been the beginning of a Scottish winter which seemed hell-bent on proving any scientist believing in the greenhouse effect a fool. Like many others in the village of Lochdubh on the west coast of Sutherland, Hamish had contracted a severe cold with all its attendant miseries of boiling head, running nose, aching joints, and monumental self-pity. Although he had not phoned anyone to tell of his misery, nevertheless, like all people in the grip of self-pity, he expected his friends to have telepathic powers.

The only bright spark in all the gloom was that he was going home for Christmas. His parents had moved to a croft house and land near Rogart. He would soon be there, with his mother to fuss over him.

He was hunched up in his bed. He was hungry and thirsty but could not be bothered getting up to get himself anything. His dog Towser, a yellowish mongrel, lay stretched out at the end of his bed, snoring happily and apparently as indifferent as the rest of Lochdubh to the long lank bundle of misery that was P.C. Macbeth.

The wind of Sutherland, always savage, had taken on a new dark intensity and boomed down the sea loch outside, bearing long snaking writhing arms of fine snow, tearing at the fabric of the house, yelling and shouting in triumph.

And then suddenly, the phone in the police-station office began to ring, sharp and insistent. He hoped no one had committed a crime. He felt too ill to cope, but if he did not attend to the matter himself, Sergeant MacGregor would have to travel all the way from Cnothan, and the peeved sergeant would then set about making trouble for him at police headquarters in Strathbane. He shoved his feet into a battered pair of carpet slippers and, sniv-elling dismally, he went through to the cold office and picked up the phone.

"Hamish," came his mother's voice, "I've got bad news."

His heart gave a lurch. "Are you all right?" he asked. "Nothing up with Faither?"

"No, no, son. It's about Christmas."

"What about Christmas?" Hamish had a bleak feeling that whatever his mother had to tell him about Christmas was not going to cheer him one bit.

"Well, Aunt Hannah's coming all the way from America. Sprung it on us at the last minute."

Hamish gripped the phone and stifled a sneeze. Aunt Hannah was a fat, loud-mouthed harridan who loathed Hamish. But she had been generous to the not-too-comfortably-off Macbeths with pres-ents of money and gifts for Hamish's little brothers and sisters. Never anything for Hamish. She loathed him and never tired of saying so.

His mother's voice grew plaintive, "So you see, son, after all Hannah's done for us and her coming all this way to see us..."

There was another long silence.

At last Hamish said bleakly, "You don't want me to come." It was not a question.

"I knew you'd understand," pleaded his mother.

"I mean, it's only this one Christmas. You could come at the New Year when she's gone."

"Aye, all right," muttered Hamish.

"I mean," coaxed Mrs. Macbeth, "you've got lots o' friends in Lochdubh. Your voice sounds funny."

"I haff got the influenza," said Hamish, his Highland accent growing more sibilant, a sure sign he was upset.

"Och," said Mrs. Macbeth with all the heartlessness of a busy mother with a large family, "you always did think you were dying when you got a wee bit o' a cold. Take some aspirin and go to bed."

Another silence. "Wass there anything else?" Hamish finally asked in accents as chilly as the police office.

"No, no, that was all. Sorry, son, but you know how Hannah is. Ever since you put that mouse down her back when you were eight, she's never been fond o' you. The new house is just fine. Rare and warm. The fires draw just grand."

"When's Aunt Hannah arriving?" asked Hamish.

"On the twentieth."

"Provided I am still alive," said Hamish stiffly, "I'll run over with your presents before then."

"Aye, that'll be great. See you then."

Hamish shuffled back miserably to bed. No one

wanted him. He was alone in the world. He was dying and nobody cared.

There came a sharp rap at the back door. He sneezed dismally and stayed where he was. Towser stirred lazily and slowly wagged his tail. The rapping came louder now, more peremptory.

Hamish's conscience gave him a nudge. He was Lochdubh's only policeman, the weather was savage, and someone out there might be in trouble. He groaned as he got up again, slung an old woollen dressing-gown about his shoulders, and made his way to the kitchen door.

He opened it and Priscilla Halburton-Smythe was borne in on a gust of wind and snow.

"Oh, it's yerself, Priscilla," said Hamish.

Priscilla, once the love of his life, until Hamish had grown heartily sick of the weight of the torch he was carrying for her, slammed the door on the storm and looked at Hamish.

"I know crime's thin on the ground here at the best of times," she said briskly, "but it's two in the afternoon and you've obviously just got out of bed."

"I am a sick man," said Hamish furiously, "but a fat lot you care. You never even thought to phone."

"How on earth was I supposed to know you were sick?" asked Priscilla. She looked slowly around the kitchen, at the cold stove, at the dirty pots and dishes piled up in the sink. "This place is enough to make anyone ill. For heaven's sake, get back to bed and leave me to clear up this mess."

"Couldn't you chust make us a cup of tea and come and sit by the bed and talk to me?" moaned Hamish.

"Nonsense. You'll feel miles better when this place is spick and span." Priscilla radiated nervous energy. She had grown thin and spare and her hair was scraped up in an untidy knot on the top of her head. Hamish thought that since her family home, Tommel Castle, had been turned into an hotel, she had not once relaxed. Although her father, Colonel Halburton-Smythe, owned the hotel, all the work fell on Priscilla. As there was excellent fishing and shooting, it was busy even in winter. It was Priscilla who saw to everything, from ordering the food and drink to soothing down the guests offended by her father's blunt manner. In an amazingly short time, she had made a success of the business, but she had lost her cool good looks and graceful movements; perpetually worried, perpetually strung up, now brittle to snapping point.

Hamish crept back to bed. "What a pigstye!" exclaimed Priscilla, following him in. "Have you fed Towser?"

"Just some o' the hard food. He doesnae like it ower-much."

"He never did like it. He likes people food. You know that, Hamish. Come, Towser."

Towser slid off the bed and crept servilely after her.

Hamish lay listening to the sound of Priscilla scrubbing floors and cleaning out cupboards and washing dishes. He felt she ought to be at his bed-side, stroking his brow, instead of going on like some sort of health visitor.

Two hours later, she crashed into the bedroom, carrying a bucket and mop and dusters. She raked out the fire, which was choked with cold ashes, piled it up with paper and wood, and set a cheerful blaze crackling. "I've run you a hot bath," she said over her shoulder. "Go and take it while I change your bed."

"I think I'm too ill to take a bath."

"Take it," she ordered, "and stop being so dis-gustingly sorry for yourself."

"Haff I complained?" Hamish gave her thin back a wounded look.

"You are exuding such self-pity, it's creeping like smoke through the whole place. *Go on!* "

Injured, Hamish stalked off to the bathroom. With quick nervous movements, Priscilla stripped the sheets off the bed and replaced them with clean ones. She dusted and vacuumed the room and then made up a flask of tea and put it, along with a cup, at Hamish's bedside.

Hamish emerged from his bath to find Priscilla waiting to settle him in bed. She neatly arranged the blankets over him and then tucked them in all round him, so firmly he felt he was in a strait-jacket.

"There's tea in that flask," said Priscilla, "and a casserole on the stove for your dinner. Towser's been fed."

Hamish wriggled his toes and eased the tight blankets a bit. The fire was roaring up the chimney and the room looked clean and comfortable and there was a delicious smell coming from the kitchen. He began to feel better.

"I'd better be off," sighed Priscilla. "I didn't mean to be here so long."

"Thank you," said Hamish awkwardly, and then blurted out before he could stop himself, "My, lassie, but you're awf'y thin."

Priscilla sat down on the end of the bed. "I know," she said. "And to think that before Daddy started the hotel, I was considering going on a diet."

"If he looks after the money this time instead of handing it over to some con man,"—Priscilla winced, said con man having been one of her boyfriends—"he should be able to take down that hotel sign soon and return to being a private landowner."

"He enjoys it all," said Priscilla sadly. "He's having the time of his life."

"Yes, I have seen him." Hamish looked at her sympathetically. "You run yourself ragged with all the management and bookings and complaints while he puts on a black tie in the evening and lords it over the guests. Then he has a few and forgets they're paying guests and is nasty to them, and you have to soothe them down."

"I'll manage."

"You don't need to," said Hamish. "Things are going just fine. Why, he could hire an experienced hotel manager and give you a break."

"But no one else could handle the guests the way I can," protested Priscilla.

"Once the colonel was paying someone to run things, he might mind his tongue. It's because you're his daughter and a woman that he treats you like a skivvy."

"It's not as bad as that." Priscilla rose to go.

"Well, it was nice of you to come and look after me."

Priscilla turned pink. "I didn't know you were ill, Hamish. There's another reason."

"Oh, aye? I should hae known," he said huffily. "Out with it."

"There's this friend of mine staying at the hotel.

She's leaving at the end of the week. She's got a bit of a problem and doesn't want to go to the police direct, if you know what I mean. She just wants some advice. Could you see her? I'd rather she told you about it."

"Oh, all right. Bring her down tomorrow. What's her name?"

"Jane. Jane Wetherby."

THE NEXT DAY, the snow stopped and a mild gale blew in from the Atlantic, turning the snow to slush. For a brief few hours, a watery sunlight shone on the choppy waters of the loch before night fell, as it does in the far north of Scotland in winter, at two in the afternoon.

Hamish was feeling considerably better. He received a phone call from headquarters at Strathbane reminding him that he was expected to stop motorists at random and Breathalyze them as part of a campaign to stop drunk driving over Christmas. Hamish, who knew every drunk in the village and solved the problem by taking their car keys away, had no intention of wasting time Breathalyzing the rest of the population.

He ate lunch, fed his hens, gave his sheep their winter feed, and then climbed back into bed with a book. He had completely forgotten about Priscilla's friend. Lulled by a glass of toddy, his eyes were beginning to close when he heard a car driving up.

Then he remembered about Jane Wetherby. It was too late to get dressed. He rose and tied his dressing-gown about him and made for the kitchen door, exuding a strong smell of whisky and wintergreen.

"Be back for Jane later," called Priscilla. "I'll leave you to it."

Hamish ushered Jane into the kitchen and then looked at her in startled amazement as she removed her coat and threw it on a kitchen chair. She was a tall woman wearing a brief divided skirt in shocking-pink wool, and her long, long legs ended in high-heeled sandals with thin patent-leather straps. Her thin white blouse plunged at the front to a deep V. Hamish cast a wild look through the kitchen window as if to reassure himself that the weather had not turned tropical, and then took in the rest of her. She had cloudy dark hair and very large grey-green eyes, a straight thin nose, and a long thin upper lip over a small pouting lower lip.

"Well, well," said Jane in a sort of breathy voice, "so you're the village constable. Why aren't you in uniform?"

"Because," retorted Hamish sharply, "I am very sick. Did Priscilla no' tell you?"

She shook her head. "Come ben, then," said Hamish sulkily. Here he was, at death's door, and Priscilla had not even bothered to tell her friend he was sick. He began to feel shaky and ill again. Priscilla had left the living-room fire set with paper and logs. He struck a match and lit it.

Jane sank down into an armchair and crossed her long legs.

"The trouble," she said, suddenly leaning forward so that her blouse plunged alarmingly low at the front, "is that you are not going the right way about curing your cold. It is the common cold, isn't it?"

Hamish, now in the armchair opposite, took out a handkerchief and blew his nose miserably by way of reply.

"It is all in your mind," said Jane. "The weather has been very cold and so you began to feel you might get one and your mind conveyed that message to the rest of your body and so you got one. Put your index fingers on either side of your head, just at the temples, and repeat after me, concentrating all the while, 'I have not got a cold. I am fit and well.'"

"Havers," said Hamish crossly.

"There you have it," said Jane triumphantly. "You have just told me what I had already guessed."

"That you were havering?" commented Hamish rudely.

"No, no. That you *want* to have a cold and make everyone feel sorry for you." She leaned back and uncrossed and crossed her legs. Embarrassed, Hamish looked at the ceiling.

"What is the difficulty you're in?" Hamish asked the lampshade. He found those flashing legs and thighs unnerving.

"I think someone might be trying to kill me."

Hamish's hazel eyes focused on her. "Did you tell someone else how to get rid of their cold?"

"Do be serious. Oh, perhaps I am imagining it, but a rock did hurtle down last week close to my head, and then there was the bathroom heater. I had run my bath and was just about to step into it when the wall heater came tumbling down, right into the bath. I called in a local builder, but he said the heater had probably just come loose as the plaster was damp."

"Did you think of telling the local policeman?"

"The local policeman is Sandy Ferguson. Have you heard of him?"

"Yes," said Hamish, remembering the famous day in Strathbane when Sandy Ferguson, drunk as usual, had told Detective Chief Inspector Blair exactly what he thought of him and had been subsequently banished to the Hebrides. "Never say you're living on Eileencraig!"

Jane nodded.

"You'd better begin at the beginning," said Hamish.

Jane looked doubtfully at the thin, red-haired constable in the old dressing-gown and then made up her mind.

"I run a health farm called The Happy Wanderer…"

"Oh, my." Hamish winced.

"Called The Happy Wanderer," went on Jane firmly, "on the island of Eileencraig. Part of the healthy regime is brisk walking. I decided to go into business for myself after my divorce two years ago. It had been pretty successful. Health farms are the coming thing. I not only teach people how to have a healthy body but how to get in touch with their innermost feelings. Do you read me?"

"Sort of."

"Well, the islanders are a clannish lot and don't like incomers, so I thought perhaps the rock thingie and the heater thingie were, well, *pranks* to scare me away. That was until I spoke to Mrs. Bannerman at Skulag, the main village, and she read my tea-leaves and she saw death in them. Someone from far away was trying to kill me, she said. That's when I began to worry about my guests."

"Paying guests?"

"No, the health farm is closed for the winter. Friends."

"Who are these friends?"

"People I invited to spend Christmas with me. There's a Mr. and Mrs. Todd from Glasgow, he's in real estate; then there's Harriet Shaw, the writer."

"Haven't heard of her," commented Hamish.

"*You* wouldn't. She writes cookery books. There's Sheila and Ian Carpenter from Yorkshire—dear, dear people, he's a farmer." Jane threw back her head and gave a merry laugh. She's practised that laugh in front of the mirror, thought Hamish suddenly. "And," said Jane, suddenly looking solemn, "there's my ex."

"Your ex-husband?"

"Yes, John. He's been working so hard. He does need a holiday."

"Who divorced whom?"

The large eyes opposite shifted away from him slightly. "Oh, we were very civilised about it. A mutual agreement. Well, there you are. What do you think?"

"Are they still there?"

"Oh, yes. After what Mrs. Bannerman saw in the tea-leaves, I felt I had to get away to meditate and heard Priscilla had fallen on hard times and so I thought I would hop over for a couple of nights just to *think*. What do *you* think?"

"First of all," said Hamish, "I believe Eileencraig

is a weird-enough place to give anyone the jitters. You're right. They hate incomers. I think the heater and the rock were plain and simple accidents. But when the villagers heard you were going to visit Mrs. Bannerman to get your fortune told, they must have put her up to giving you a fright. That, in my opinion, is all there is to it."

She leaned forward and the blouse plunged alarmingly again. "Do you know," said Jane in that breathy, sexy voice of hers, "you are a *most* intelligent man." She threw back her head and gave that practised merry laugh of hers again. "I was so edgy that when Priscilla told me about you, I was going to invite you to come back with me for Christmas and bribe you with the promise of an old-fashioned dinner of turkey and mince pies."

Hamish sat stricken. Then he said carefully, "On the other hand, I cannot help thinking about my Aunt Hannah, her that lives in San Francisco."

"Yes?"

"She always swore she would neffer set foot in Scotland again, but a wee woman in the Chinese quarter told her fortune and said she would soon be going on a long journey to her native land. She forgot all about it, until one day she found she had booked a plane flight home to Scotland. Then there wass ma cousin Jamie..."

Jane's mouth fell a little open as she gazed at him.

"Yes, Jamie," said Hamish in a crooning voice. "He was at this game fair and a gypsy woman had a caravan there. Jamie and his friends had a wee bit too much to drink and they urged Jamie to have his tea-leaves read. Into that black caravan he went, laughing something awful and telling that gypsy woman it was all a load of rubbish. But she read the leaves."

"And?" urged Jane, who was goggling at him.

"And the gypsy woman said, 'Laugh ye may, but look out for your life. Next week, someone is going to try to kill you.' Well, Jamie, he thought she was trying to get revenge because he had laughed at her, but the very next week"—Hamish lowered his voice to a whisper—"he was in Aberdeen, looking for work on the rigs, and someone mugged him."

"No!"

"Oh, yes, and stuck a knife in his side. He's lucky to be alive."

"I have never jeered at the paranormal," said Jane. "You may think me foolish, Hamish, but I am begging you now to come with me. Can you get any leave?"

"I happen to be on leave as from tomorrow," said Hamish, "but with this cold…"

"I have very good central heating," said Jane, "and you will be looked after like a king."

"Seeing as how you are a friend of Priscilla's, I'll force myself to go," said Hamish.

WHEN PRISCILLA ARRIVED to pick Jane up, she looked amazed to hear that Hamish intended to travel to Eileencraig with Jane and stay there for Christmas. "I'll talk to you later," said Priscilla.

Jane's eyes fell on Towser. "No dogs," she said.

"Perhaps I can take Towser." Priscilla looked doubtful. "But I'll talk to you later, Hamish."

After they had gone, Hamish poured himself a celebratory whisky. He had nearly blown it. If he had not invented those tales about his relatives and the tea-leaves, he might not have had a comfortable Christmas to look forward to.

Priscilla arrived that evening, looking cross. "What on earth are you up to, Hamish Macbeth? Jane told me some rubbish about tea-leaves and I was leaving it to you to talk her out of it. Besides, what will your family think?"

"They don't want me," said Hamish. "Aunt Hannah's coming over from the States and that means I have to stay away. She cannae stand me. Och, I forgot the presents for the family. I was supposed to take them over at the end of the week."

He looked at Priscilla pleadingly.

"All right! All right!" she said impatiently. "I'll

take Towser *and* the presents over to Rogart. In fact, I'll do it tomorrow and get it over with. There's bad weather forecast. The wind's turned to the east and all that slush is beginning to freeze like mad. I can't help feeling guilty about letting you trick Jane into that invitation, but seeing as how you've got a holiday and nowhere else to go, and seeing as how Jane is simply loaded, I suppose it should be all right."

"You're always rushing." Hamish tried to take her coat. "Sit down for a bit."

"No, no, I daren't. We've got a party of Spanish aristocrats. They speak perfect English, which is something Daddy refuses to understand, so he shouts at them and thinks if he puts *h* in front of everything, he's speaking Spanish. You should hear him roaring, 'H'everything h'okay?' "

She threw her arms about him and gave him an impulsive hug. "Be good, Hamish. Have a merry Christmas."

"Merry Christmas," echoed Hamish as she hurtled out of the door and banged it behind her. He could still feel the warmth of her thin body for a few moments after she had gone, and into his mind came slight, sad, bitter-sweet memories of the days when he had loved her so much.

*   *   *

THE SUN CAME up at ten in the morning to shine over a glittering icy landscape, a glaring yellow sun which forecast high gales to come. True to her promise, Priscilla collected Towser and the presents and set out on the long road to Rogart while Hamish climbed into Jane's Range Rover and headed down the coast. Jane said that a fishing boat would take them out to the island, as no passenger ferry was due there for another week. She was wearing a short leather jerkin over another short skirt and a pair of black leather thigh-boots. She discoursed at length on her innermost feelings as she drove competently down the winding twisty roads beside the glittering sea. If anyone ever issued a press handout about innermost feelings, it would read rather like Jane's conversation, reflected Hamish. She suffered, she said, from low self-esteem and a perpetual feeling of insecurity, and Hamish wondered if she really felt anything much at all. She seemed to be reciting something she had read about someone else rather than talking about herself. He wished suddenly he had not taken her up on her invitation. It would have been fun if he could have gone to his parents', instead, with Priscilla. He had not seen much of Priscilla of late. She was always busy, always rushing.

PRISCILLA DROVE UNDER the shadow of the towering Sutherland mountains. Great gusts of wind tore at the car and then the snow began to fall. She switched on her headlights and leaned forward, peering through the driving snow, watching the road in front uneasily as it became whiter and whiter. She heaved a sigh of relief when at last she saw the orange street lights of Lairg ahead. Not far to go.

The road from Lairg to Rogart is quite a good one, although it seemed, that afternoon, to be disappearing rapidly under the snow. Priscilla stopped outside Rogart and studied a map Hamish had drawn for her. The Macbeths' house was above the village, up on the hills.

She was feeling tired with the strain of driving so long in the howling blizzard. She crawled up the hill road at the back of Rogart, peering anxiously in front of her. And then, with great relief, she saw the telephone-box that Hamish had drawn at a crossroads on his map. The entrance to the croft was a few yards up on the left. The car groaned and chugged its way along. She had almost decided she would need to stop and get out and walk when she dimly saw the low shape of a white croft house. Hoping she was not driving across the front garden, she drew up outside the door and sat for a moment, rubbing her tired eyes.

The kitchen door opened and the small round

figure of Hamish's mother appeared. "It's yourself, Priscilla," she cried in amazement. "And the dog! Where's Hamish?"

"It's a long story," said Priscilla, climbing out of the car and walking with Towser into the welcoming warmth of the house. There seemed to be Macbeths everywhere, both large and small, and all with Hamish's flaming-red hair.

"I'll just leave Towser and the presents from Hamish, and then I'd better get back," said Priscilla, after explaining where Hamish was.

"Nonsense," said Mrs. Macbeth. "Sit yourself down, lassie. You're no' going anywhere tonight."

She was hustled into the living-room and pressed down into a battered armchair by the fire. A glass of whisky was put into her hand. Priscilla realised for the first time in months that she was tired, bone-tired. Her eyes began to droop and the empty glass was gently removed from her hand. Soon she was fast asleep.

"Did ye ever see such a mess o' skin and bone?" said Mrs. Macbeth, looking down at Priscilla. "It's fattening up that lassie needs. She cannae go anywhere until the roads are clear. And it's just as well. Hamish said that faither o' hers was a slave-driver, horrible wee man that he is. I think we'll keep her here for a bit until she gets some rest."

Mr. Macbeth smiled at her vaguely and retreated behind his newspaper. He had given up arguing with his wife exactly two weeks after they were married.

"I DO RELY on Priscilla for advice," Jane was saying as she drove competently along a stone jetty. "We'll just wait in the car until we see the boat coming, Hamish, and then I'll garage it in that lock-up over there. Yes, Priscilla. So cool. Such a relaxing girl. Oh, there's the boat."

Hamish climbed out of the warmth of the Range Rover and shivered on the jetty. Small pellets of snow were beginning to blow through the rising wind. He looked over the sea and experienced a slight feeling of uneasiness, almost dread, and wished he had not come.

Chapter Two

From the lone shieling of the misty island
Mountains divide us, and the waste of seas—
Yet still the blood is strong, the heart is
Highland,
And we in dreams behold the Hebrides!

—Sir Walter Scott

The lights of the fishing boat which was to carry them to Eileencraig bobbed closer across the water. Hamish, out of uniform, pulled his tweed-coat collar up against the biting wind. Jane, he noticed, was wearing her jacket open. There might be something to this health-farm business after all, he thought.

The fisherman was a gnarled little man with a sour expression. Jane hailed him gaily, but he jumped nimbly onto the jetty and began to tie the rope around a bollard, ignoring her completely, as did his second in command, a pimply-faced boy with pale eyes, a wet mouth, and an incipient beard.

"Angus is quite a character," said Jane, meaning the fisherman and giving that merry laugh of hers again. She and Hamish went on board, Hamish carrying her heavy suitcase and his own travelbag. The two-man crew cast off and the boat bucketed out over the rough sea. Hamish went down below to an oily, stinking little engine room furnished with two smelly berths and a dirty table. He sat on one of the berths. The youth scrambled down and went into the galley and put a kettle on the stove, which was lurching about on its gimbals.

"What's your name?" asked Hamish.

"Joseph Macleod," said the boy. He began to whistle through his teeth.

"Is Mrs. Wetherby in the wheel-house?" asked Hamish.

"Naw, herself is oot on the deck."

"In this weather?"

"Aye, her's daft. There's worse coming." The boat lurched and bucketed but the boy kept his balance, swaying easily with the erratic motion. "Right bad storm inland. Heard it on the radio."

Hamish thought uneasily of Priscilla. They were on the west coast. The storm had been driven in from the east. He hoped she was safe.

Jane clattered down to join Hamish, her face shining with good health. "Marvellous sea," she said. "Waves like mountains."

"I can feel them, and that's enough." Hamish, still seated on one of the berths with the raised edge of it digging into his thighs, looked queasily at Jane. "It's a wonder you got them to bring the boat out in this weather."

"I pay well." Jane lay down on the other berth and raised one booted leg in the air to admire it.

Hamish had to hand it to Jane. It was a dreadful crossing and yet she prattled on as if lying on a sofa in her own living-room. The little fishing boat crawled up one wave and plunged down the next and then wallowed about in the choppy trough at the bottom before scaling another watery mountain. The boy left the kettle and started to work the pumps, for sea water was crashing down the companion-way. The air was horrid with the sound of wind and waves and the groanings of the boat as it fought its way to Eileencraig.

Hamish's cold felt worse. His forehead was hot and there was a ringing in his ears. Jane's presence was claustrophobic. There was too much of everything about her, thought Hamish dizzily. Too much length of black-booted leg, too much cleavage, and too much of that breathy, sexy voice that rose remorselessly above the storm.

"The reason for the divorce," Jane was saying, "was that we both needed space. It's very important to have space in a marriage, don't you think?"

"I wouldn't know," replied Hamish, "not being married myself."

Jane's large eyes swivelled round like head-lamps turning a corner to focus on him. "Everyone to their own bag," she said cheerfully. "Have you a lover?"

"I am not a homosexual."

"Then why aren't you married? I mean, you're over thirty, aren't you? And anyone over thirty who is not married is either a homosexual or emotionally immature."

"It could be argued that divorce is a sign of emotional immaturity," said Hamish. "Inability to make a go of things once the first fine careless rapture has died down."

"Why, Hamish Macbeth, you are straight out of the Dark Ages!"

Hamish got up and clutched at a shelf for support. "Going to get a breath of air," he said, and scurried up the iron stairs before Jane could volunteer to accompany him.

It was still wild, but the great seas were dying. He went into the wheel-house. "Nearly there," grunted the fisherman.

Hamish peered through the spray-blotched window. "Can't see anything but darkness and water."

"Ower there." The fisherman pointed to the middle west. Hamish strained his eyes. He had never been to Eileencraig. Then, all at once, he saw lights in the blackness, lights so low that he seemed to be looking down on them. He was to find out later that a large part of the center of the very flat island was below sea-level. The sea was calming. Somewhere far overhead, the wind was tearing and shrieking, but down below, all was suddenly still, an eerie effect, as if Eileencraig, like a sort of aquatic Brigadoon, had risen from the sea.

Jane appeared on deck, obviously looking for him. He went out to join her. The boat cruised into a wooden jetty. There were little knots of people standing on the jetty.

As they disembarked, Hamish carrying the luggage, he gave them a cheery salute of "Afternoon," but they all stared back at Hamish and Jane without moving, like sullen villagers in some long-forgotten war watching the arrival of their conquerors. There was something uncanny about their stillness, their watching. Their very clothes seemed to belong to an older age: the women in black shawls, the men in shiny tight suits. They stood immobile, watching, ever watching, not moving an inch, so that Hamish and Jane had to walk around the little groups to get off the jetty.

Hamish had once had a murder case in a Sutherland village called Cnothan. There, the inhabitants were anything but friendly but would have looked like a welcoming committee compared to these islanders.

Jane strode to where an ex-army jeep was parked and swung her long legs into it, and Hamish climbed in beside her after slinging the luggage into the back. "Horrible old thing," commented Jane, "but sheer extravagance to leave anything more expensive lying around. They'd just take it to pieces."

"Out of spite?" Hamish looked back at the islanders on the jetty, who had all turned around and were now staring at the jeep, their black silhouettes against the jetty lights, like cardboard cut-outs.

Jane drove off. "Oh, no," she shouted above the noise of the engine. "They're rather sweet really. Just like naughty children."

"Why on earth do you stay in such a place?"

"It is part of the health routine to have walks and exercise in such a remote, unspoiled part. My guests love it."

They probably would, thought Hamish, cushioned as they were from the stark realities of remote island life.

"And just smell that air!"

As the jeep was an open one, there was little else Hamish could do but smell the air. The road wound through the darkness, the headlights picking out acres of bleak bog at every turn.

Jane swerved off the road and drove over a heathery track and then along the hard white sand of a curve of beach. "There it is," she called. "At the end."

Floodlit, The Happy Wanderer stood in all its glory, cocking a snoot at the simple grandeur of beach and moorland. It had been built like one of those pseudo-Spanish villas in California with arches and curved wrought-iron balconies, the whole having been painted white. A pink curly sign, "The Happy Wanderer," shone out into the blackness.

It fronted right on the beach. Jane pulled up at the entrance.

"Home at last," she said. "Come in, Hamish, and I'll show you to your room."

The front door led straight into the main lounge. There was a huge fireplace filled with blazing logs; in front of it stood several chintz-covered sofas and armchairs. The room had a high arched wooden ceiling and fake skin rugs on the floor; a fake leopardskin lay in front of the fire, and nylon sheepskins dotted, like islands, the haircord carpet. Several modern paintings in acid colours swore from the walls. There was no reception desk, no receptionist, no pigeon-holes for keys and letters.

Jane conducted him down a corridor that led off the far end of the lounge and threw open a door with the legend "Rob Roy" on it. The room was large, designed in a sort of 1970s interior decorator's shades of brown and cream, with a large vase of brown-and-cream dried flowers on a low glass table. There was a double bed and a desk and several chairs and a private bathroom. A bad painting of Rob Roy waving a broadsword and standing on his native heath looked down from over a strictly ornamental fireplace, and a bookshelf full of women's magazines was beside the bed. There was, however, no television; nor a phone.

"Where is everyone?" asked Hamish.

"I suppose they're in the television room as usual. Odd, isn't it? I mean the way people can't live without television."

"Can I have my key?" asked Hamish.

Again that merry laugh, which was beginning to grate on Hamish's nerves. "We don't have keys here, copper. No need for them. We're all one big happy family. I try to make it as much like a private house as possible."

"Yes, and I suppose if anyone does pinch anything, they wouldn't get very far," commented Hamish cynically. "There's no phone, so I suppose there's no room service. Any chance o' a cup of tea?"

Jane looked at him seriously. "Do you know that tea contains just as much caffeine as coffee?"

"Coffee would do just fine."

"You don't understand. *Both* are bad for you. But come and meet the others when you're ready."

Hamish sighed and sat down after she had left. He wondered whether he was supposed to change into black tie for dinner and then decided that the rugged people who came to remote, wind-swept health farms probably sat down in shorts and T-shirts.

He had a hot bath, changed into a clean shirt, sports jacket and flannels, swallowed two aspirin, and went in search of the others.

By following the sound of the six-o'clock news, he located the television room. Only one person looked up when he entered, a woman who had been reading a book. The rest were staring at the box. Jane then burst into the room. She had changed into a sort of white leather jump suit, the gold zip pulled down to reveal that cleavage. "Drinks in the lounge," she called.

A tetchy-looking man who held a remote control switched off the television. The small party rose stiffly to their feet. Hamish thought that they all, with the exception of the book-reading woman, looked as if they had been gazing at the television set since Jane had left on her visit to Priscilla.

A drinks trolley was pulled up near the fire. "I'll introduce our newcomer," said Jane. "This is Hamish Macbeth, a friend of Priscilla's—you know Priscilla, the one I went to see. Hamish, first names will do. Heather and Diarmuid, Sheila and Ian, Harriet and John."

Hamish's eyes roved over the group. Which was Jane's ex? He found the woman who had been reading had joined him. She had been introduced as Harriet. This then was Harriet Shaw, the cookery-book writer. She was a stylish-looking woman in her forties with a sallow, clever face made almost attractive by a pair of large humorous grey eyes.

"Jane told me you write books," said Hamish.

"Yes," said Harriet. "I came up here in the hope of getting some old Scottish recipes from the islanders."

Hamish looked rueful. "I wouldn't bank on it. You'll find they dine on things like fish fingers and iced cakes made in Glasgow. Help me out. Who are the others? First names are not a help."

"Have a drink first," said Harriet.

"In a moment. I would really prefer a cup of tea. Jane seems down on caffeine, though. I thought she would have frowned on alcohol."

"She seems to think it all right in moderation. Well, the couple drinking gin and tonics are Heather and Diarmuid Todd. He's in real estate. She's a self-appointed culture vulture."

Diarmuid Todd was an attractive-looking man; that is, to anyone who liked the looks shown in tobacco advertisements. He had thick brown wavy hair and a pipe clenched between his teeth. He was smiling enigmatically and staring off into the middle distance. Despite the heat of the lounge, he was wearing a chunky Aran sweater with blue cords and boat shoes without socks.

His wife, Heather, looked older. She had blackish-brown hair and was wearing a pink jump suit with high heels. But her figure was lumpy and she looked like a parody of Jane, whom she obviously admired immensely. She had a doughy face set in lines of discontent.

"And Tweedledum and Tweedledee, that's Ian and Sheila Carpenter."

Ian and Sheila Carpenter were both roly-poly people with fat jolly faces and fat jolly smiles. They were flirting with each other in a kittenish, affectionate way.

"The small, bad-tempered man is Jane's ex, John Wetherby."

John was well-groomed, slightly plump, looking as if he had been reluctantly dragged from his office. He was wearing an immaculately tailored pin-striped suit, a shirt with a white separate collar and striped front, and an old school tie.

"He's a barrister," said Harriet. "So what do *you* do?"

Hamish hesitated. It was obvious that Jane did not want anyone to know he was a policeman. "I work for the forestry," he said.

Heather Todd, who had come up to them, caught Hamish's last remark. Her eyes bored insolently into his. "Good heavens," she said, "where did Jane pick *you* up?"

"In Lochdubh, on the mainland," said Hamish amiably.

Heather's voice was Glaswegian, although it would take a practised ear to register the fact. Among the middle classes of Glasgow it had become unfashionable to try to affect an English accent, the painful result of that effort usually coming out as what was damned not so long ago as Kelvinside, the name of one of the posher areas, where glass came out as "gless" and path as "peth." The new generation of middle-aged, middle-class snobs affected a transatlantic drawl ("I godda go") but occasionally throwing in a few chosen words of Scottish dialect to show they were of the people, there being nothing more snobbish than a left-wing Glaswegian who longed for the days when that city was a dump of slums and despair instead of having its present successful image. These same snobs talked about "the workers" and their rights frequently, but made sure they never knew one, short of indulgently telling some barman when they were slumming to "buy that wee fellow in the cap a drink."

"Do you realise what you and your like are doing?" demanded Heather.

"No, tell me." Hamish looked around, wondering whether he could ask Jane to relent and fetch him a cup of tea. There did not seem to be any staff.

"Covering the Highlands with those ghastly conifers, and all so that rich yuppies in England can get a tax shelter."

"Forestry is no longer a tax shelter," pointed out Hamish. "There arnae that many jobs in the Highlands, and forestry's a blessing."

"Well, that's not the way *I* see it," said Heather, casting her eyes about her to draw an audience from the rest. "The massacre of the flow country in Sutherland, the damage to the environment..." Her hectoring voice went on and on. Hamish did not like the dreary new pine forests that covered the north of Scotland, but someone like Heather always made him feel like defending them.

"I'll find you a cup of tea," said Harriet's voice at his ear, and she tugged at his sleeve. They slipped quietly away while Heather continued her lecture, her eyes half-closed so that she could better enjoy the sound of her own voice, which went on and on.

Harriet led him into a sterile-looking kitchen where everything gleamed white under strips of fluorescent light.

"I bet it's herb tea," said Hamish, looking gloomily about.

"No, real tea. I've been in charge of the kitchen while Jane's been away." Harriet opened a cupboard and took down a canister of tea and then plugged in an electric kettle.

"Never tell me Jane does all her own cooking," Hamish said more in hope of being contradicted than anything else.

"Not while the hotel is running." Harriet heated the teapot and spooned in tea-leaves. "Women come in during the day to do the cleaning and make the beds. But for us, her friends, she does do the cooking."

"Health stuff?" asked Hamish.

"Well, yes, but you only have to suffer for the

next few days. I'm doing a traditional Christmas dinner, and, of course, tonight's dinner."

"Which is?"

"Very simple. Sirloin steak, baked potato, peas and carrots, salad. Before that, soup; and after that, butterscotch pudding." She filled the teapot.

"And were you all friends before you met up here?"

"No," said Harriet. "We're all new to each other. In fact, I was very surprised to get Jane's invitation. We're not that close. I felt I was putting on too much weight—oh, about four years ago—and went to a health farm in Surrey. Jane was there, slim as ever, but finding out how a health farm was run. We talked a lot and then met once or twice in London for lunch. How did you meet her?"

"I'm a friend o' a friend o' hers," said Hamish. "That's all. I had nowhere to go this Christmas and she asked me along."

The grey eyes regarding him were shrewd. "And that's all? You're not Jane's latest?"

"Hardly," said Hamish stiffly, "with her husband present."

"Her *ex*-husband. But that wouldn't stop Jane. Anyway, she's made a go of things here. Of course, she imports a lot of staff during the tourist season, chef, masseur, waitresses, the lot. The Todds, that's Heather and Diarmuid, were paying guests, and so they're now here as non-paying friends. The same with the Carpenters."

"More like acquaintances than friends."

"Exactly. Off with you. I've got to prepare dinner." Harriet took down a tray and put teapot, cup and saucer, sugar and milk on it, handed it to Hamish, and shooed him out.

Hamish returned to the lounge, carrying the tray. He was feeling much more cheerful. He liked Harriet Shaw.

But no sooner had he taken off his sports jacket and tie, for the room was hot and there did not seem to be any rigid dress code, and established himself in an armchair, than Heather Todd bore down on him and stood over him, her hands on her hips. "Are you a Highlander?" she demanded.

"Yes," said Hamish, carefully pouring tea and determined to enjoy it.

She threw back her head and laughed. It was a copy of that laugh of Jane's, which always sounded as though Jane herself had copied it from someone else.

"A Highlander, and yet you are prepared to contribute to the rape of your country."

Hamish's eyes travelled up and down her body with calculated insolence. "Right now, I've never felt less like raping anyone or anything in ma life."

Heather snorted, and one sandalled foot pawed the carpet. "What of the Highland clearances?" she demanded.

"That wass the last century."

"Burning the poor Highlanders' houses over their heads, driving them out of their homes to make way for sheep. And now it's trees!"

"I hivnae heard o' one cottager being turned out to make way for a tree," said Hamish, trying to peer round her tightly corseted figure to see if Jane or anyone else looked like coming to his rescue.

"What have you to say for yourself?" Heather was asking.

"What I haff to say," said Hamish, his suddenly sibilant accent betraying his annoyance, "is that when the Hydro Electric board was burying whole villages under man-made lakes, your sort never breathed a word. Now that it iss politically fashionable to bleat about the environment, it's hard for folks like me to believe you give a damn."

Heather did not listen to him. He was to learn that once launched, you could say what you liked, she never heard a word. Irritated, he rose and pushed past her and sat on the other side of the room.

He was joined by John Wetherby. "I could kill that woman," said John. "Pontificates from morning till night."

"Well, maybe her husband will do the job for you." Hamish looked longingly at the tea he had been forced to abandon.

"Him! That wimp. Have you seen him pass a mirror? He stops dead-still and gazes longingly at himself like a man looking at a lover."

"Let's talk about something else," said Hamish. "What brought you here?"

"I am Jane's ex-husband."

"Aye, just so, but what brought you?"

"Oh, I get you. I couldn't believe she'd made such a go of things. When we were married, she was always full of hare-brained schemes to make money. That's how I got her to agree to a divorce. I said I would put up the money for this place if she agreed. I thought she would be back after a year, asking me to bail her out, but not a bit of it."

"And weren't you embarrassed about seeing her again . . . after the divorce, I mean?"

He gave a cackle of laughter. "You don't know Jane. Have you heard her psycho-babble yet? There's not one idea in that head of hers that doesn't come straight out of a woman's magazine. An article on 'How to Be Friends With Your Ex' was one she enjoyed a lot. Are you the latest amour? She occasionally liked a bit of the rough stuff."

Hamish was too amazed to feel insulted at this

bit of blatant snobbery. "Did she have affairs when you were married?"

"Yes, she said we had become sexually stagnant and went out to experiment." His voice grew reflective. "It was that hairy truck-driver I couldn't take."

Hamish gave John Wetherby a prim look of startled disapproval and rose and moved away. The Carpenters, surely, would be safe company. Sheila was reading a book and Ian was sipping a large whisky and smiling vaguely at nothing.

He sat down next to Ian. "Topping place," said Ian, looking around.

"I hear you're a farmer," said Hamish. "Funny, I wouldn't have thought farmers would go to health farms. Although, come to think of it, maybe that's not true. I just had a vague idea that perhaps health fanatics went in for it."

Ian patted his round stomach complacently. "Sheila keeps up with all the fads. We each lost five pounds when we were here in the summer. Of course, we put it all back on again the week we got home. Didn't we, sweetie?"

"Mmm?" Sheila was buried in a book with a pink cover called *Love's Abiding Passion*. Her lips were moving slightly and she was breathing heavily through her nose.

And then Heather was before them. "What are

you reading, Sheila?" she demanded. Sheila gave a little sigh and held up the book so that Heather could read the title.

"My dear, dear Sheila," said Heather, shaking her head. "Surely you can find something better than that pap?"

"It's a marvellous book," said Sheila, her fat cheeks turning pink.

Heather suddenly snatched it out of Sheila's hand and flicked over the pages and then gleefully read aloud. " 'There was a tearing sound and the thin silk cascaded at her feet. He thrust his hot body against her naked one and she could feel his aroused masculinity bulging against her thigh.' I ask you, Sheila, how can you bear to read a book like that?"

Sheila snatched it back and heaved herself out of the sofa and waddled from the room. Her husband stood up and glared at Heather. "It's better than the works of Marx any day."

"It would considerably improve your wife's mind to read Karl Marx."

"Yah!" said Ian. "What d'you lot think about the fall of Communism in Eastern Europe, hey?"

"That was not real communism," said Heather. "Real communism..."

"Stuff it, you old crow," said the farmer and left the room with the same waddling walk as his wife.

Hamish felt like running after him and shaking his hand.

Before Heather could speak to him again, he darted for the door and let himself out into the night. The high wind of earlier in the day had descended to ground level and was tearing and shrieking and moaning along the shore, where seals lay at the edge of the crashing waves, their curious eyes gleaming pink from the neon sign of The Happy Wanderer.

The wind was cold. Hamish wished he had remembered to put on his jacket. Priscilla often called him a moocher. He hugged his thin body against the bite of the wind. He should have stayed where he was in Lochdubh. He could imagine someone saying they would like to strangle Jane, but no one would really think of doing it. There was not enough real about the woman to encourage great love or great hate. And that marriage of hers! When John had been talking about that truck-driver, Hamish had felt slightly sick.

His cold would get worse if he stayed outside. He walked back in. Jane was standing talking to Heather. Heather was not hectoring Jane about anything but looking at her with open-mouthed admiration and hanging on every word.

"Is there a telephone?" Hamish asked Jane.

"There's one in my office you can use. It's over

there," said Jane, pointing to a door on the right of the lounge.

Hamish walked over to where she had pointed. A ceramic sign on the door said "Jane's Office" and was decorated by a wreath of painted wild flowers.

The office was strictly functional; large steel desk, steel filing cabinets, two easy chairs for visitors.

Hamish sat behind the desk, picked up the phone and dialled Tommel Castle, now called Tommel Castle Hotel. He recognised the voice of Mary Anderson, a local girl, who operated the hotel switchboard. "Can I speak to Priscilla?" he asked.

"Herself is not back," said Mary. "She went to Rogart."

"Is the storm bad?" asked Hamish, trying to blot out pictures of a car upended in a blizzard by the side of the road with a woman and a dog lying beside it.

"Oh, it's real bad. That's Hamish, isn't it?"

"Yes. Has she phoned?"

"No, but they got it worse over there than here, so folks are saying. Maybe the lines are down."

Hamish thanked her, put down the receiver, then lifted it again and dialled his parents' home.

His mother answered. "Is Priscilla there?" demanded Hamish, his voice sharp with anxiety.

"Aye, she's here. But you cannae talk to her, son."

"Why?"

"The poor lassie's still fast asleep by the fire. My, Hamish, she used to be the most beautiful girl I've ever seen, and now she's nothing but skin and bone. She cannae leave. She'll need to stay the night. I'll let her sleep a bit and then give her a good supper and put her to bed."

"Have you the room?"

"Och, yes, we'll put a cot bed in the girls' room. How's yourself?"

"I'm just fine."

"Is it a grand place?"

"Well, it's a health farm, sort of mock-Spanish villa."

"On Eileencraig! My, my."

"Dinner," called Jane, putting her head round the door.

"I've got to go, Ma," said Hamish quickly. "I'll phone tomorrow."

He said goodbye and sat for a moment looking at the phone. What on earth would the elegant and fastidious Priscilla make of his noisy, easygoing family?

He rose then and went out through the lounge to the dining-room. It was panelled in pine wood. Several small tables had been put together to make a big one and it was covered by a red-and-white-checked cloth and decorated with candles in wine bottles. A stag's head ornamented one wall, and Hamish noticed to his surprise that it was fake. He hadn't known that such a thing existed. Jane probably did not approve of bits of real animal being used, hence the fake head and the synthetic skins on the lounge floor.

Dinner was excellent and Hamish could only be glad that he was seated between the Carpenters and therefore protected by their bulk from Heather. Also, to his relief, conversation at dinner was innocuous. Jane was explaining that they would all go for a walk along the shore in the morning and then, after lunch, take a walk inland while there was still some light. Hamish enjoyed the excellent meal washed down with some good claret. He began to feel mellow. It was not going to be such a disaster after all. But he should show some gesture toward earning his keep.

As soon as dinner was over, he asked Jane to show him that bathroom heater.

Jane let him into her bedroom, through a door emblazoned with the legend "Sir Walter Scott." It was furnished pretty much the same as the one allotted to Hamish, except that there were two bookshelves stuffed with women's magazines instead of one.

He went into the bathroom and examined the heater carefully and then stood back and looked at the ceiling.

There was a patch of damp and black mould beginning to form on it. He was sure the builder had been right and that the heater had fallen off the wall because of the damp. In fact, probably the whole structure of the health farm needed to be treated for damp, but to tell Jane that at this early date would make him feel more of a fraud than he was and so he murmured non-committally that he would take another look at it on the following day, and that he would probably start his investigations by going to see Mrs. Bannerman.

Jane stood very close beside him. "I see what Priscilla means," she said. "You *are* very competent."

Hamish shied and took a nervous step back.

"How did you meet Priscilla?" he asked.

"It was at a party in London," replied Jane. "Such a boring party, we decided to leave early and went to a bar for a drink and got talking. We had a few lunches after that."

"And when did you last see her?"

"About three years ago, and then I heard this summer that her father had gone bust and turned the castle into an hotel."

Hardly a friendship, thought Hamish. "Shall we

join the others?" he said, easing around her and making for the door.

Jane looked a little disappointed but followed him out. "Pity," she murmured. "I've never had a policeman before." Or rather, that's what Hamish thought she'd said.

The rest of the guests were back in the television lounge and grouped around the set. It was a talk show. A famous film star told everyone how he had got off the booze, and he was followed by a famous romantic novelist.

Heather's eyes narrowed. "Just look at that silly woman. It gars me grue to see creatures like that making all that money producing rubbish."

Sheila flushed and Hamish noticed that she slid the romance she had been holding on her lap down the side of the chair.

"Here, wait a minute," said Harriet crossly. "I may only write cookery books, but I do know something about romance writers. To be successful you can't write down, and very few of them make big money."

Heather sniffed. "Money for old rope, if you ask me. And the historical ones are the worst. I doubt if they even open a history book."

"Well, it's the romance that sells it, not the historical content," said Harriet soothingly. "For example, if I wrote a book about the French Revolution, I would describe the tyranny and horror and how the storming of the Bastille was only to get at the arsenal. There were only seven people freed, you know. Now your true romance writer would see it more through the eyes of Hollywood. Thousands of prisoners would be released while the heroine, dressed in rags, led the liberators. Great stuff. I really sometimes wonder if the less romance writers know, the better.

"Or, for example, I would describe a shiekh of the desert as a fat little man with glasses and a dish-towel on his head. Your true romance writer would have a hawk-eyed Rudolph Valentino character in Turkish turban and thigh-boots. It's a harmless escape."

"Harmless!" Heather snorted. "It's even got women like poor Sheila here stuffing her mind with rubbish."

"For heaven's sake," said Harriet crossly, "you watch the most awful pap on television, day and night. There was a programme on Channel Four last night about some Hollywood producer who does soft-porn horror films and who was treated by the interviewer as a serious intellectual. Anyone who writes popular literature, on the other hand, is treated like a charlatan, and do you know why,

Heather? It's because the world is full of morons who think they could write a book if only they had the time. You're just jealous!"

"Yes, if you're so bloody superior," said John Wetherby, "why don't *you* write a book, Heather?"

Heather looked at them like a baffled bull. Hamish guessed it was the very first time during her visit to the island that she had been under attack.

"Aren't we all getting *cross?*" cried Jane. "Switch the goggle box off, John, and we'll all have a game of Monopoly instead."

Hamish was then able to see another side to Jane, the good-business/hostess side. She flattered Heather by asking her questions about the latest shows in Glasgow as she led them through to the lounge and spread out the Monopoly board on the table. She teased Sheila charmingly on having such a devoted husband and said she ought to write an article and tell everyone her secret. She congratulated Harriet on a beautiful meal and told Diarmuid, Heather's husband, that he was so good-looking she was going to take some photographs of him to use on the health-farm brochure.

They all settled down in a better humour to a long game of Monopoly and nobody seemed to mind very much when Heather won.

Hamish at last went off to bed. The bed was

comfortable and the central heating excellent. He wondered why Jane had seen fit to have extra wall heaters put in all the bathrooms, and then reflected that she was a clever-enough business woman to cosset her guests by seeming to supply them with a rigorous regime of exercise outside while pampering them with warmth and comfort indoors.

He was sure no one was trying to kill her. And yet, he could not shake off a nagging feeling of uneasiness. He put it down, after some thought, to the fact that he disliked Heather intensely and had been shocked by John's revelations about his marriage. He would avoid them as much as possible. Harriet Shaw, now, was worth spending time with, and on that comfortable thought he drifted off to sleep.

SHEILA CARPENTER SAT in front of the dressing-table in the room called Mary of Argyll which she shared with her husband. She wound rollers in her hair while her husband lay in bed, watching her.

"I could kill her," said Sheila suddenly.

"Who?"

"Heather, of course."

"I'll do it for you, pet. Don't let her bother you. She's not worth it."

"Petty, stupid snob," said Sheila with uncharacteristic viciousness.

*   *   *

"WHO IS THAT long drip of a Highlander?" demanded John Wetherby. Jane shrugged. She was putting away the Monopoly pieces in their box. "Just some friend of Priscilla's."

"You can't fool me. For your benefit, your dear friend Heather told me this Macbeth was your latest."

"It's not true," said Jane. "And Heather would not say anything malicious like that."

"Oh, no? She's a first-class bitch and I feel like bashing her head in."

Jane studied him seriously and then said in a voice of patient reason, "You must stop this irrational jealousy, John. It's not flattering or even sexually motivated. It is simply based on totally irrational masculine possessiveness. It said in an article I was reading the other day . . ."

"Pah!" shouted John and stomped off to his room.

DIARMUID TODD SAT at the dressing-table and trimmed his fingernails. His wife, Heather, was reading *The Oppression of the Working Classes in a Capitalist Society*. She read as far as page 2 and then put the book down. "What do you think of our Jane's latest?"

Diarmuid paused, and then continued working on

his nails with all the single-minded fastidiousness of a cat at its toilet. "Who do you mean?" he asked.

"Why, that Highland chap, Hamish something-or-another."

Her husband put away the scissors in his leather manicure case and then took out an orangewood stick and began to clean his nails. "I don't think he's anything other than a friend, Heather, and I hope you haven't been going around saying anything else."

His usually bland Scottish voice had a slight edge to it. "Maybe not," said Heather. "Jane's a very attractive-looking woman but hardly a man-eater. There's something, well, sexless about her."

She patted the springy waves of her permanently waved hair with a complacent hand before picking up her book again.

The stick snapped in Diarmuid's suddenly tensed fingers and he threw his wife a look of pure and unadulterated hatred.

HARRIET SHAW CREAMED her face vigorously and then slapped at what she feared might become a double chin one of these days and wished she had not come. The Carpenters were sweet, but Heather was too much to take. Thank goodness for that Hamish fellow. He was charming and quite attractive in a way with his fiery-red hair and hazel eyes. Better stick with him till the holiday was over or she would end up killing Heather. She amused herself before falling asleep by thinking out ways to get rid of Heather and then how to dispose of the body, until, with a smile on her lips, she fell fast asleep.

Chapter Three

Though by whim, envy, or resentment led,
They damn those authors whom they never read.

—Charles Churchill

To Hamish's surprise, breakfast, cooked by Jane, turned out to be an excellent meal, although he missed not having any tea or coffee. It consisted of toast and low-cholesterol margarine, fresh grapefruit, muesli, and a large glass of freshly squeezed orange juice.

The breakfast was marred only by the seething emotions around him. Jane had appeared wearing pink denim shorts with a bib front over a white-and-pink-checked blouse and walking boots in tan leather. She was shortly followed by Heather, wearing exactly the same outfit.

Heather's face was flushed and angry and Diarmuid looked sulky. They had just had a row. The normally placid Diarmuid had suddenly snapped that if Heather thought Jane sexless, then why did she try to dress like her? It only made her look like a fright. And certainly Heather did look awful, having rolls and bumps of flesh where Jane had none, and fat white hairy legs, Heather believing that to shave one's legs was merely pandering to masculine sexism. Jane looked at Heather as she entered and something for a moment glittered in the depths of her eyes and then was gone.

Sheila had carried her romance to the breakfast table and was reading it, occasionally darting nasty little looks at Heather, and her husband also darted angry little looks at Heather, so that the round Carpenters looked more like twins than husband and wife.

John Wetherby was glowering at his breakfast. He was wearing a V-necked pullover over a blue shirt and a tightly knotted tie, grey flannels, and walking shoes, his idea of suitable wear for a hiker.

Jane rose and addressed them at the end of the meal. "This will not do," she said gaily. "There is a nasty atmosphere and we should all be having a lovely, lovely time." She lifted a box and put it on the table. "I have here a supply of balloons, thread, and pencil and paper. Now, I suggest we each write down our resentments, blow up our balloons, and carry them outside and watch them all float away!"

"Oh, for God's sake, Jane," snapped her ex-husband. "Be your age."

"Don't be stuffy," said Heather. "Sounds like fun. Come on, Sheila, get your head out of that trash." She gave that laugh copied from Jane. "It's like watching a rather nice little pig with its head in the trough."

"Watch your mouth, you rotten bitch," shouted Ian.

"I know what it is," cried Jane, holding up her hands. "We need some fresh air to blow the cobwebs away. Forget about the balloons. Where's your Christmas spirit? Get your coats and *off* we go."

They all meekly rose to their feet. "I don't think I can bear this," said Harriet to Hamish.

He smiled down at her. "I have to go over to the village this morning, and maybe there's a bar there..."

"I'll come with you," said Harriet. "Don't tell the others. We'll just join the end of the crocodile and then veer off."

Jane set out at the head of the group. Her voice floated back to them. "Let's sing! All together now. 'One man went to mow...'"

"Come on," said Hamish to Harriet as the group straggled along the beach behind Jane.

The air was warmer than the day before, but a

howling gale was still blowing. Snatches of Jane's singing reached the ears of Hamish and Harriet as they made their way inland and onto the road that led to the village. The rising sun was low on the horizon, curlews piped dismally from the heather, and sea-gulls crouched on the ground, occasionally taking off to battle with the gale.

They tried to talk but at last fell silent, for the shrieking wind meant they had to shout. Harriet was wearing a tweed jacket and matching skirt. Her short brown hair streaked with grey was crisp and curly. She walked with an easy stride by Hamish's side. Hamish was happy. The silence between them was companionable, tinged with a conspiratorial edge prompted by their escape from the others.

They turned a bend in the road and in front of them stood a very battered old Fiat truck, parked in the middle. They made their way around it and stopped short. A small man was sitting at the side of the road in front of the truck, weeping bitterly.

"Hey," cried Hamish, crouching down beside the forlorn figure. "What's your trouble?"

"It iss him," said the man, raising a tear-stained face and jerking a gnarled thumb in the direction of the truck. "He iss out to kill me."

Hamish got up, and motioning Harriet to stand well back, he went quickly to the truck. There was

no one in the cabin and nothing in the back but barrels of lobster.

He loped back and sat down on the road beside
the man and said coaxingly, "Now, then, there's no
one there. Who are you talking about?"

"Him!" said the little man passionately, and
again that thumb jerked at the truck. "Can't you see
him, sitting there, watching me?"

The truck-driver was probably only in his forties,
but hard weather and a hard life made him appear
older. Like most of the islanders, he was small in
stature. He had a weather-beaten face. Sparse grey
hairs clung to his brown scalp.

Harriet bent down and shouted above the tumult of
the wind, "But there is not a soul about except for us."

"Wait a bit." Hamish held up his hand. "Do you
mean the *truck* is trying to kill you?"

"Aye, the beast! The beast. Wass I not loading the
lobsters and did he not back into me and try for to
tip me into the sea?"

"And did you not have the brakes on?" said
Hamish cynically. "What is your name?"

"Geordie Mason."

"Well, listen, Geordie, stop your havering. I am
Hamish Macbeth, and this is Harriet Shaw. We're
going into Skulag. I'll hae a look at your truck and
drive it for ye."

Geordie rubbed his eyes with his sleeve. "Wid ye dae that? Himself will no' mind. It's jist me he cannae thole."

Hamish drew Harriet aside. "It'll save us a walk," he said. "I'm sure the wee man is harmless. Probably been at the methylated spirits."

Hamish climbed into the driving-seat, Geordie sat next to him, and Harriet on the other side. It was an old-fashioned bench seat, and so it could take the three of them comfortably.

Hamish turned the key in the ignition. The engine gave a cough and remained silent. "Ye've got to tell himself it's no' me that's driving." Geordie had recovered from his grief and seemed almost proud of demonstrating the bloody-mindedness of his vehicle.

Harriet stifled a giggle. "All right," said Hamish amiably. "Does he have a name?"

"He's an agent o' the deil, no' a pet."

"Why he?" asked Harriet. "I mean boats and planes and things like that are she."

"I jist ken," said Geordie, folding his arms and glaring through the windscreen.

"Oh, Fiat truck," said Hamish Macbeth, "this is your friend speaking. This is not your master, Geordie Mason. We're going to Skulag, so be a nice truck and get a move on."

He grinned as he turned the key in the ignition, a grin that faded as the old engine roared into life.

"Told ye so, but would yis listen?" demanded Geordie with gloomy satisfaction.

Hamish drove steadily down the road, reflecting that he should be taking better care of Harriet. Perhaps Geordie would start seeing green snakes or spiders before they reached the village. And yet the man did not smell of drink.

"Is there a pub of some kind?" he asked.

"Aye," said Geordie. "Down at the hotel, The Highland Comfort, next tae the jetty."

The village of Skulag was a small cluster of low houses standing end-on to the sea, some of them thatched in the old manner with heather. There was no one to be seen as they rattled down the cobbled main street. Hamish parked neatly in front of the hotel, which was on a small rise above the jetty. It was a two-storeyed white-washed building, originally built in the Victorian era as a holiday home for some misguided Glasgow merchant who had survived only one holiday summer before putting the place up for sale. It had been an hotel ever since.

Inside, apart from a hutch of a reception desk, the rooms leading off the hall still bore their Victorian legends of "Drawing-Room," "Smoking-Room," and "Billiard-Room."

Hamish, who had been in such hotels before, opened the door marked "Drawing-Room" and there, sure enough, was the bar along one wall. Along the other wall was a line of glass-and-steel windows overlooking the jetty.

"What are you having?" asked Hamish. "I'd sit at a table over at the window, Harriet. I doubt if the natives are friendly." He nodded towards the line of small men in caps who were propping up the bar. They looked back at him with sullen hostility.

"A whisky and water," said Harriet.

Hamish ordered two whiskies and water and then carried them over to a table at the window.

"There's that poor mad truck-driver," said Harriet.

Hamish looked out. The truck was where he'd left it, parked on the rise. A little below, at the entrance to the jetty, stood Geordie, leaning forward against the force of the wind and trying to light a cigarette.

And then, in front of Hamish's horrified eyes, the truck began to creep forward and Geordie was standing in a direct line of its approach.

Hamish struggled with the rusty catch of the window and swung it open. "Geordie!" he yelled desperately. "Look out!"

Geordie looked up, startled. The truck stopped dead.

"Wait a minute," said Hamish to Harriet.

He ran outside the hotel and straight up to Geordie. "You'd better have the brakes on that truck of yours checked," he shouted against the screaming of the wind.

Geordie shrugged. "What's the point? Anyway, himself stopped when he heard you."

Hamish went back to the truck and climbed inside the cabin. The keys were still in the ignition. He switched on the engine and put his foot gently on the accelerator. Nothing happened. The brakes held firm.

He switched off the engine and got down and walked to the front of the truck. There was no explanation why the thing had suddenly stopped. It was parked on a slope, it had started moving, and it had stopped when he called.

He shrugged and went back into the bar to join Harriet.

"Odd," he said. "Did you see that?"

"He should get it checked," said Harriet. "A good mechanic would sort the trouble out in no time."

The men at the bar were staring at both of them and talking rapidly in Gaelic. "What are they saying?" asked Harriet.

"My Gaelic's a bit rusty," said Hamish, "but they are saying, I gather, some pretty nasty things about

Jane. That wee man there with the black hair is saying she should be driven off the island and the other one is saying someone should kill the bitch."

"How awful! Why are they so nasty about her? Jane's harmless."

"I think it's just because they are nasty people," said Hamish. He shouted something in Gaelic in a sharp voice and the men relapsed into sulky silence.

The door to the bar opened and a large policeman lumbered in. He had a huge round fiery-red face and small watery eyes. Those eyes rested briefly on Hamish and then sharpened. He marched up to their table.

"Whit are you doing here?"

Harriet looked from Hamish to the policeman in surprise.

"Holiday, Sandy," said Hamish briefly.

"At The Happy Wanderer?"

Hamish nodded.

"You need to pit on weight, man, no' lose it." Sandy looked cynically down at Hamish's thin and lanky form. "Wait a minute. The place is closed. She's got her friends there."

"One of which is me," said Hamish equably.

"You're up tae something." Sandy looked mulish. "And if I find you're poaching on my territory, I'll phone Strathbane and have ye sent home."

"Do that." Hamish gazed up at him blandly.

Sandy muttered something, turned and threw a longing look at the bar, and then slouched out.

"What was all that about?" asked Harriet. "Have you a criminal record?"

Hamish shook his head. "I'll tell you the truth if you promise to keep it to yourself. I am the local copper in a village called Lochdubh on the west coast of Sutherland. Jane asked me to come because she was afraid someone was trying to kill her."

"Oh, the bathroom heater. But that was an accident. But of course I won't tell anyone who you are."

"Jane herself thought it an accident but she went to a Mrs. Bannerman in this village and got her fortune told. This Mrs. Bannerman told her that someone from far away was trying to kill her. Jane had also just missed being hit by a falling rock. She was worried it might be one of you. I plan to see Mrs. Bannerman this morning. Would you like to come along?"

Harriet grinned. "Lead on, Sherlock. This is all very exciting."

"Now that you know the truth about me," said Hamish, "tell me what you think of the other guests. Let's start with the horrible Heather."

"I've met types like Heather on visits to Glasgow," said Harriet. "She seems to spend an awful lot on entertaining any visiting celebrity she can, running a sort of Glaswegian salon. She's a fairly rich, old-fashioned Communist, looking for another totalitarian regime to worship now that Stalinism has been finally discredited. Says she was brought up in the Gorbals when it was a really horrible slum and tells very colourful stories and I am not sure I believe any of them. Quotes Sartre in very bad French. Refers to celebrities by their first names, Rudi being Rudolph Nureyev, things like that. Adores Jane and is jealous of her at the same time. Jane has no political affiliations that I know of, but she hails from an old county family, and that's enough for a snob like Heather. Jane's maiden name is Bellingham. Her pa owns a minor stately home in Wiltshire and Heather keeps hinting she'd like an invitation. Heather is the kind who hangs around the private section of stately homes on view to the public in the hope that one of the family will emerge and recognise one of their own kind."

"I don't get it," said Hamish. "And her a Communist!"

"When it comes to social climbing, such as Heather never lets politics get in the way, hence her friendship with Jane. Hates romance writers. There's still plenty of first-class romance writers around, but she reserves her venom for what used to be called novelettes, you know, the laird and the country girl, or the advertising exec and the secretary. It's still the laird and the country girl or whatever, but with lashings of sex thrown in. Nothing too vulgar. Lots of euphemisms. She says all their royalties should be taken from them by the government and given to writers' workshops to help the up and coming intellectual. She's about fifty-three. I would say Diarmuid is a bit younger.

"I don't think there's much more to Diarmuid than what you see. He is a supremely vain man and yet appears proud of his unlikeable wife. That atmosphere between them this morning was totally new. He's in real estate, so he can't be doing too well at the moment with the fall in the market.

"John Wetherby. Well, that seems to have been an odd marriage. He delights in running Jane down. I sometimes wonder if she had affairs to score off him. I sometimes wonder if she had any affairs at all. She is a good business woman, but I can't seem to find anything deeper than what you see on the surface. John is a successful barrister, opinionated to the point of smugness. Why he accepted Jane's invitation I do not know. I cannot see one trace of affection in his manner towards her. I gather he is a trifle mean and Jane told me he probably jumped at the idea of a free holiday."

Hamish winced and said quickly, "And the Carpenters?"

"He's got a farm in north Yorkshire. At first when I saw them flirting with each other and cooing at each other, I thought that marriage looked too good to be true, but I think they are a genuinely nice and rather innocent couple."

"And Harriet Shaw?"

She smiled and he liked the way her eyes crinkled up. "Widow, no children, writes cookery books which are moderately successful. Gets money from occasional television programmes and cookery articles for magazines. Wonders what she is doing on this bleak island talking about suspects to a policeman."

Hamish laughed. "Drink up and let's see this Bannerman woman. I'll just find out at the bar where she lives."

Harriet waited for him at the door. "Last cottage at the end of the main street, on the left," said Hamish, returning from the bar. "Let's get out of here. You could cut the hostility with a knife."

As they were leaving, a housemaid, about to descend the stairs, saw them, and retreated quickly.

"Nobody loves us," mourned Hamish.

They walked down the main street, and women appeared outside their cottages and stood watching them. One approached them, a small woman with a fat white face. She caught hold of Hamish's sleeve and began to talk to him urgently in Gaelic. Hamish listened patiently and then shook himself free and walked on.

"What did she say?" asked Harriet.

"She said that Jane's a whore. There was a bad storm the other week and two of the fishermen were washed overboard. They say it's God's punishment for having a scarlet woman on the island. Jane's been here for two years now. Doesn't she notice any of this? She got me here to protect her because she thinks someone's trying to kill her. Well, after listening to that woman, I've decided that maybe someone is, and if she doesn't shut up shop soon and leave, they'll drown her."

"How did she know who we are?"

"They saw me arriving with her off the boat. Two men left the bar while we were there. The fact that I spoke to them in Gaelic would go round the village in minutes. Here's this Bannerman woman's place."

She opened the door before they could knock. "I knew you wass coming," she intoned. Harriet looked startled, but Hamish grinned and said, "Phoned you from the bar, did they?"

"Come in," she said rather huffily. They entered a low, dark parlour. Mrs. Bannerman ushered them into chairs and sat facing them.

She was in her thirties, guessed Hamish, and was

wearing what looked like a 1960s Carnaby Street outfit: peasant blouse, flowered skirt, bare feet, and beads. Her hair was long and straggly and she had a thin, unhealthy-looking face and small black eyes. He saw with surprise that her neck was dirty. It was not often one saw a dirty neck these days.

She leaned forward and looked into Hamish's eyes. "Well, Hamish Macbeth," she crooned, "and what haff you to say to me?"

Harriet started, thinking the woman really had psychic powers, but Hamish glanced at the phone in the corner of the room. His conversation with Sandy would have been overheard. Sandy had a loud voice. Sandy had probably dived into the bar after they left and the barman had phoned Mrs. Bannerman with the details.

"I am here on holiday," said Hamish, "but I would still like to know why you told Mrs. Wetherby that someone was trying to kill her or going to kill her."

"I saw death," moaned Mrs. Bannerman, "right there at the bottom of the cup. I felt a great blackness come ower me."

"I think you were put up to it, that's what I think," said Hamish, becoming tired of all this mumbojumbo, particularly as he sensed that Mrs. Bannerman was enjoying herself hugely. "And where is Mr. Bannerman?"

"Dead and gone," she wailed.

"Dead of what?"

"Died innis bed," she snapped, her voice momentarily coarsening and losing its Highland accent.

"Where?"

"Ah'm I bein' accused o' anything?" demanded Mrs. Bannerman angrily.

"Only that I think you're a fraud."

"Whit?" She rose to her feet in a rage. "Get oot o' ma hoose and go and bile yer heid!"

"That didn't get you very far," said Harriet once they were outside.

The Fiat truck rattled along the main street and came to a stop in front of them. "If you're going back, I'll gie ye a lift," called Geordie.

"May as well," said Hamish. They climbed into the cabin.

"Going all right now?" asked Hamish.

"Aye," said Geordie. "I gave him a wee bit o' oil, not that he needs it, but he aye likes a treat."

Hamish stifled a groan. "Tell me about Mrs. Bannerman," he said. "She's not an islander, is she?"

"Naw, herself's frae Glasgow. Come up here, must hae been about five years ago."

"So why all the hostility to Mrs. Wetherby and none to her?"

"She doesnae go around dressed in them short

skirts," said Geordie. "Besides, she knows her tea-leaves and ye go careful wi' someone like that."

"Did that silly woman tell you that your truck was trying to kill you?" asked Hamish.

"Don't be daft," said Geordie. "The truck telt me."

Hamish gave him an uneasy look, wondering just how deranged Geordie was.

"And what of Mrs. Bannerman's husband?"

"Doing a stretch for g.b.h. in Barlinnie Prison."

"What's g.b.h.?" asked Harriet.

"Grievous bodily harm," said Hamish but with his eyes still fixed curiously on the driver. "How did you find that out?"

"Her mither arrived frae Glasgow last year on a visit. Rare gossip that woman wass."

"And who did Bannerman attack?" pursued Hamish.

"I don't know," said Geordie. "Will ye leave me tae drive himself in peace?"

They travelled the rest of the way in silence, thanked Geordie when they got off at The Happy Wanderer, and went inside to find the others quite resentful that they had decided to go off on their own.

Hamish asked Jane if he might use her phone and then went into the office and phoned his mother. "Priscilla gone?" he asked.

"No," said his mother. "She can't really travel. The roads are still bad. She started fretting about her father and the guests, so I told her to get on to Mr. Johnson at the Lochdubh Hotel. They're closed down for the winter. I told her to ask him to go up and offer his services for the Christmas period and ask a high price. The colonel will want his money's worth out o' Johnson, but he'll respect someone he's paying a lot for."

"Good idea. But I'll bet she won't do it."

"She already has," said his mother triumphantly.

"My! Can I speak to her?"

"No, son, she's out sledging with the children."

They talked for a little and then Hamish rang off, trying to imagine Priscilla sledging with his brothers and sisters. Hamish had been an only child for many years, and then, when his mother was in her forties, she had begun to produce brothers and sisters for him, three boys and three girls. This largely explained Hamish's unmarried state, for it was a Highland tradition that the eldest should stay unmarried and help to support the family. He sent everything he could home and had learned to be thrifty, as well as expert at cadging free meals.

Lunch was an edgy affair. He wondered what on earth was up when he entered the dining-room and felt the weight of the silence. Harriet told him afterwards, as they all set out for the afternoon walk with Jane, that Sheila had decided to carry her lunch into the television room in order to watch the midday showing of the Australian soaps. Heather had lectured her on the stupidity of this pastime and had even gone in and switched off the television. Sheila had burst into tears and thrown her first course of vegetable soup at Heather's head.

They marched inland, Jane striding out in front, the rest trailing behind. The sky was darkening above and the sun was sinking low on the horizon and then, just before darkness fell, Jane stopped and pointed to the west. It was an awesome sight. They were almost at the centre of the island. It was below sea-level. Out to the west, it looked as if the whole of the Atlantic were about to come charging down on them. "How terrifying to look *up* at the sea," said Harriet. She moved closer to Hamish and he put an arm around her shoulders and she leaned against him briefly, then straightened up and disengaged herself, her cheeks pink.

The exercise had revived everyone's spirits and there was a sort of silent agreement not to quarrel. John Wetherby caught up with Jane and they headed back to the hotel. Hamish noticed that John and Jane were talking like old friends.

Dinner was pleasant. Then television destroyed

everything. Heather wanted to watch a production of *King Lear* in modern dress; the rest wanted to watch *Cheers* and *The Golden Girls*. Heather lectured them bitterly on the folly of watching rubbish produced by American imperialists. Jane put it to a vote and the American imperialists won. Heather stalked off to bed.

Immediately the atmosphere lightened. Diarmuid stayed to watch the comedies and laughed as hard as the rest. But when it was over, John Wetherby suddenly glared at his ex-wife, who was sharing a sofa with Diarmuid. Jane had changed into a short miniskirt and blouse. "Pull your skirt down, for God's sake," he snapped. "You're showing everything."

Jane blushed furiously. It was the first time Hamish had seen her really put out. Then she gave that merry laugh and suggested they all move through to the lounge for drinks.

Hamish retired to bed early. Once more he felt gloomy. Once more he wished he had never come.

THE NEXT DAY was a hell of low cloud and driving rain. House-bound, the guests idled about. Hamish began to read some of Jane's magazines to pass the time. He found a serial in *Women's Home Journal* that was extremely good and rifled through the back numbers until he had got the whole book and settled down comfortably to read.

"I'm going out for a walk," called Jane. "Anyone coming?"

Diarmuid half-started to his feet but his wife pulled him back down. No one else moved.

"Then I'll go myself," said Jane. She was wearing a bright-yellow oilskin. She hesitated at the door and looked at John Wetherby. He grunted and picked up his newspaper and hid behind it.

Jane walked out.

The day dragged past. But at four in the afternoon, Hamish realised it was pitch-black outside and Jane had not returned.

"Where's Jane?" he asked suddenly.

"Probably in the kitchen," said John. He was now playing chess with Diarmuid.

"I'll look," said Harriet quickly.

She came back after about ten minutes. "She's not in her room, and not in the kitchen, not anywhere. Her oilskin's missing."

Hamish got his own coat and made for the door. "Wait a bit," called Harriet. "I'm coming with you."

They collected torches from a ledge beside the door and made their way out into the howling gale. "Where would she go?" shouted Hamish.

"The beach," said Harriet. "She usually walks on the beach when she's on her own."

They walked rapidly along the beach. The tide was coming in and great waves fanned out at their feet. Hamish was cursing himself. He had taken his duties too lightly. He should never have let her go off on her own. "You'd better take my hand," he shouted at Harriet. "I don't want you getting lost as well."

Harriet had a warm, dry hand. Despite his anxiety, Hamish enjoyed the feel of it.

And then the wind dropped, just like that, as it sometimes does on the islands, with dramatic suddenness. There was no sound but the crashing of the waves.

They stopped and listened hard.

Harriet squeezed his hand urgently. "Listen! I heard something. A faint cry."

"Probably a sheep."

"Shhh!"

In the pause between one wave and the next, Hamish heard a faint call. It was coming from someplace in front of them. It could be a nocturnal sea-bird, but it had to be investigated. They walked slowly on, stopping and listening.

And then they heard it, a cry for help. Hamish swung the torch around and its powerful beam picked out a pillbox on a bluff above the beach, one of those pillboxes built out of concrete during the Second World War. Dragging Harriet after him, he ran towards it. "Jane!" he called.

"Here!" came the faint reply.

A door had been put on the pillbox, quite a modern door with a shining new bolt. Hamish jerked back the bolt and Jane Wetherby tumbled out. As Harriet comforted her, he shone the torch inside. It was full of old barrels and fishing nets and bits of machinery. Someone was using it as a store-house.

He went back to Jane. "What happened?" he asked.

"I was walking along the beach and I saw the pillbox door open. It was the first time I had seen it open. It was a bit nosy of me, but I went to have a look inside. Nothing but nets and things. And then someone pushed me and I went flying inside and the door was slammed and bolted behind me. Those village children, no doubt."

"Are you all right?" asked Harriet anxiously.

"Yes, fine. I wasn't scared. I just didn't want to spend the night in there. It was getting so cold."

The night *was* bitter cold. Hamish walked back, worried. A less healthy and robust woman than Jane, locked up there and left for, say, twenty-four hours before she was found, might have died of exposure. "Who owns that pillbox, or rather, who uses it?" he asked.

"I don't know," said Jane.

Back at the health farm, and after Jane had answered all the guests' questions, Hamish took her aside and said it was time he had a quiet talk with her, perhaps when the others had retired for the night.

"Come to my room," said Jane.

Hamish eyed her nervously and scratched his red hair. "What about the kitchen?" he suggested, and Jane agreed. Twelve o'clock was decided on.

The guests retired early. Hamish lay reading more magazines until midnight. Then he left his room and went through to the kitchen. He pushed open the door.

Jane was standing by the table in the centre of the room. She was wearing a black, transparent nightie over a suspender belt and black stockings and very high-heeled black shoes. "Good evening, copper," she said.

Chapter Four

And sadly reflecting,
That a lover forsaken
A new love may get,
But a neck when once broken
Can never be set.

—William Walsh

Hamish stood in the doorway, his eyes averted. "I'll chust wait here, Jane, while you go and put something on."

"Oh, come *on*, Hamish," she said breathily, and moved towards him.

"I'll wait for you in the lounge," said Hamish crossly. "Don't you dare come near me until you make yourself decent." And he stalked off, as stiffly as a cat.

Jane appeared in the lounge five minutes later. She had put on a housecoat that covered her from throat to heel. "Better?" she queried, tossing her hair.

"Much better," said Hamish. "Now, lassie, chust you sit yerself down and tell me what on earth you were playing at."

"Hamish Macbeth, I shouldn't need to spell it out for you. A bit of fun."

He shook his head in amazement. "That's hardly the way to go about it. What would you have felt like in the morning?"

"Much better," said Jane earnestly. "Sexual intercourse is a very healthy exercise and good for the skin."

"So's jogging. Jane, Jane, have you no feelings at all? Do you never feel rejection when a pass is turned down, shame when it isn't?"

Jane looked at him in a puzzled way, one finger to her brow. Then her face cleared. "Calvinism. That's it!" she cried. "You have been brought up to have your mind warped by repressive religion."

"And you haff been brought up to have your mind warped by women's magazines. I thought all this free love was out of fashion anyway," said Hamish wearily. "We're not getting anywhere. I must tell you flat that when John told me about your affairs, I felt sick."

"Which one in particular?" asked Jane curiously.

"Some truck-driver."

"Oh, that. The fellow was as queer as a coot. I only brought him around to annoy John."

"Why?"

"He kept accusing me of having loose morals and he hurt me by his constant criticism of what he called my dizzy mind, so I decided to get my revenge. The laugh is that I was faithful to him right up till the divorce."

"Then why try to get me into bed?"

"Oh, well, I thought if I did that, there would be a certain something between us and John would notice..."

Her voice trailed away.

"I'm not going to discuss this any further," said Hamish. "I am here to do a job and I didn't do it very well by letting you wander off on your own. I'll go into the village tomorrow and report it to the local policeman. I couldn't phone tonight. The man would be drunk as usual. Have you any idea if it was a man or a woman who pushed you?"

Jane shook her head.

"The pillbox is quite near the hotel. Haven't you seen anyone coming and going—using it?"

"Oh, yes," said Jane, "some little man."

"Description?"

Jane shrugged. "They all look the same to me, small and bitter and prematurely old."

"So you *do* know there's a lot of hostility against you on this island? Why on earth do you stay amidst such hatred?"

"Hamish, I barely see them, and they're cheerful enough when the health farm opens up to visitors because it means cleaning and serving jobs for the local women. They never did like me. There's been a sort of intense hatred started up just recently."

"The Bannerman woman?"

"I can't see how she can have anything to do with it. She's always been one of the women who've actually talked to me when I've gone into the village. Look, Hamish, I've made a success of this place. People who wouldn't dream of going to a health farm in the home counties come up here. It has a romantic interest and I attract walkers and outdoor types as well as those who want to lose weight. I showed that ex-husband of mine I could do it and made him eat his words."

"I'll let you know how I get on with my investigations tomorrow," said Hamish. "Good night."

She threw him a look, half-mocking and half-appealing. One hand toyed with the long zip at the top of her housecoat and Hamish was frightened she meant to pull it down and fairly scampered from the room.

*   *   *

THE NEXT DAY, he made his way towards the village. He had hoped Harriet might have wanted to accompany him, but that lady had gone out walking with Heather, of all people.

Once again, he came across Geordie and his truck stuck on the road. Geordie, Hamish had decided, staged these breakdowns for some mad reason of his own, and so he ignored Geordie's moanings and wailings and offered to drive him. He had been unable to borrow Jane's jeep because it was insured to cover only her driving.

The truck started amiably enough. "He likes you," said Geordie, shaking his head. "An odd beast."

"Forget about the truck," said Hamish. "Who uses that pillbox on the beach?"

"Angus Macleod. Him and his son have a fishing boat. It wass the wan that brought yourselfs over."

"Well, last night, someone pushed Mrs. Wetherby into that pillbox and bolted the door. She could have died of exposure."

"Och, it's all right," said Geordie. "Angus wass in the bar last night and he wass saying he would let herself out at midnight when he had given her a rare fright."

"I'll be seeing Angus, then," said Hamish grimly.

"Ye won't be able to dae that. Himself took the boat out this morn."

Hamish stopped the truck. Geordie screeched, "He disnae like tae be stopped fur no reason at all."

"Forget the truck. Listen. Do you hate Mrs. Wetherby?"

"Naw, I hivnae the time to hate anybody what with bringing the lobsters over frae the west and collecting the goods for people to deliver when the ferry comes in."

"Well, she's hated nonetheless. When did it start?"

"Och, nobody likes incomers, and the wimmen are fair scandalized with the leg show she puts on, but it must hae been recently they all started cursing and blinding. Don't know what started it."

"Well, I'll find out." Hamish turned the key in the ignition. Nothing happened, not even a choke. "I telt you he didnae liked to be stopped fur no reason," said Geordie patiently.

"I'm fed up wi' your nonsense." Hamish opened the door. "I'm walking."

He slammed the door behind him and strode off down the road. "Come back!" screeched Geordie's voice. "He's following you!"

Hamish turned around, and with a feeling of superstitious dread, he saw the truck rolling silently towards him. He stopped and the truck stopped beside him. He climbed in, checked the brakes, turned the key in the ignition, and the engine roared to life.

He drove silently into Skulag, vowing that once he had a bit of time, he would find a mechanic to check Geordie's truck.

The police station was locked. Hamish leaned on the bell for a considerable time until at last the blear-eyed constable, still in his pyjamas, answered the door.

"And they call *me* lazy!" marvelled Hamish.

"What d'ye want?" growled Sandy.

"I want you to put on your uniform and go and charge Angus Macleod with assault."

"He's awa'."

"Well, when he comes back."

Sandy looked at him with contempt. "You mean, for pushing thon Wetherby woman into the pillbox? That's naethin's but mischief. Look, Macbeth, I'm no' going tae arrest anyone. When I first got here, I arrested two o' the fishermen for stealing the council's wire wastebaskets off the jetty to use as lobster pots. The islanders gathered around the polis station calling for ma' blood and I had to climb out on the roof and sit there most o' the night. If you think I'm arresting Angus for a little bit o' fun, think again." He slammed the police-station door in Hamish's face.

Hamish strolled thoughtfully along the jetty. He could phone Strathbane and report Sandy, but he did not want to do that. There would be a full-scale inquiry and he, Hamish, would be made to look ridiculous. Besides, all the islanders, he was sure, would gang up and swear Angus had been with them all day. He saw one of the fishermen, and remembering Geordie's truck, asked him if there was a mechanic on the island.

The man stood for a long time and then decided to reply. "There's Bert Macleod down the village. He does the MOTs and things like that," meaning the annual Ministry of Transport checks on all vehicles over three years old.

"And where does he live?"

"Opposite Mrs. Bannerman."

Hamish walked along the village street, all too aware of the twitching curtains. Mrs. Bannerman was working in her patch of front garden. She saw him and scurried inside.

Opposite her house on the other side of the street was a cottage with a shed at the side, with the legend "A. J. Macleod, Motor Mechanic," above the door.

He went inside. There was a pair of legs in greasy overalls sticking out from under a car.

"A word with ye," called Hamish.

The man wriggled out and scrambled to his feet.

"Are you any relation to Angus Macleod?" asked Hamish.

"His brither," said Bert sullenly.

"He's in bad trouble. He's assaulted Mrs. Wetherby."

"It wis jist a joke and Sandy won't be touching him."

"No, but I'm a policeman, and if Sandy doesn't do anything about it, I can report him to headquarters and he'll be taken off the island and you'll get a replacement who won't put up wi' your nonsense."

Bert, a small man with weak eyes behind thick-lensed glasses, blinked up at Hamish. He jingled some change in his overall pocket and looked sly.

"We could aye come to an arrangement," he said in a wheedling voice.

"Aye, maybe we could. Do you ken Geordie Mason, him wi' the haunted truck?"

"O' course."

"Did the MOT, did you?"

"Last year. Naethin' up wi' it."

Hamish looked at him cynically. He knew there were garages that would pass any old vehicle as being sound, provided the price was right.

"If you want me to leave Angus and Sandy alone, you'll do this. Tell Geordie I've said there is something wrong wi' his truck and get it in here and take it apart and make sure it's sound."

Bert pushed back a filthy cap and scratched his head. "It won't mind that," he said. "Geordie says it likes a bit of attention."

"You're all crazy," said Hamish in disgust. "Just see to that truck."

On the road back, he turned his mind to the problem of who could possibly have started the hatred for Jane Wetherby. Mrs. Bannerman? Someone from the health farm? Did anyone from the health farm talk to the islanders? They had all been there two weeks before his own arrival, time enough to do damage. He would need to ask Harriet. The thought of Harriet Shaw cheered him immensely. The wind had dropped as he neared The Happy Wanderer, and snow began to fall in large feathery flakes. He stopped, amazed. He could not ever remember having seen a white Christmas. Usually it snowed a bit before Christmas and a lot after Christmas. Perhaps this too would fade away before the twenty-fifth.

A Christmas atmosphere seemed to have fallen on Jane's guests at last. They were all helping her trim a large synthetic tree in the lounge and hang decorations. Even John Wetherby was laughing as he stood on top of a ladder and tried to reach up to put the fairy on top of the tree.

When the tree was finished, Hamish took Jane aside and told her the result of his investigations.

Jane clapped her hands in delight. To Hamish's horror, she called out, "Listen, everybody! Isn't Hamish clever? He went into Skulag and found out that it was Angus Macleod, a fisherman, who pushed me into that pillbox."

John Wetherby slowly turned round. He had been bent over a box to start bringing out the tinsel and paper decorations with which to decorate the rest of the lounge and dining room. At Jane's words he straightened up abruptly and swivelled to face Hamish.

"You reported this to the police, of course," he said sharply.

"Of course," said Hamish, dreading what was going to come next.

"Then why hasn't the policeman been out here to take Jane's statement?"

"Because Angus told everyone he only did it to give Jane a fright and that he was going to let her out at midnight. Sandy refused to charge him."

"Well, he'll bloody well have to charge him. All Jane has to do is make a complaint of assault and see he does his duty."

"It's not so easy," said Hamish. "All the islanders will gang up and say that Angus was in their sight all day."

"Forensic tests," barked John.

"They wouldn't get anywhere," said Hamish wearily, "that is, if Strathbane even bothered to send anyone out here. Footprints? The tide's been up as far as the entrance to the pillbox, not to mention the howling wind sweeping any marks clear. Fingerprints? Of course Angus's would be on the bolt, for it's where he stores his stuff."

John Wetherby stared at him long and hard and then a smile curled his lips. "I've got it," he said softly. "You're a copper yourself. Not a private detective, not even a police detective. Who else, I ask you, would wear boots like that?"

Hamish looked miserably at his feet. He was wearing an old tweed sports jacket, checked shirt, and plain tie and cords. But on his feet were his regulation boots. They had been broken in long ago and were very comfortable, and the thrifty Hamish had seen no reason to waste money on shoes when the state could supply him with footwear.

Harriet Shaw's eyes travelled quickly from face to face. There was a stillness in the room. Heather was frankly goggling, Diarmuid was looking enigmatic as usual, the Carpenters were leaning against each other, plump shoulder against plump shoulder, but someone had let out a startled exclamation, quickly stifled. Which one had it been?

"All right," said Hamish. "But I *am* on holiday."

"It was that bathroom heater," said John, rounding on Jane. "You silly cow. How like you to get so paranoid over a mere accident."

"At least he found out who shut me in the pill-box," said Jane quietly. "Now can we all just go ahead and try to have a decent Christmas?"

Whether it was Jane's remark, whether it was the presence of a policeman among them, or whether it was because Christmas was approaching was hard to tell, but at least the next few days passed almost in tranquillity. Hamish was surprised that Heather went to great lengths to keep out of his way. He had expected to have lectures from her on the fascist police.

Harriet, too, appeared to be avoiding him. When Hamish taxed her with it, she smiled and said she was too busy catching up on some writing in her room. He took refuge in reading articles in the women's magazines collected by Jane. They ranged from the supremely sensible to the downright ludicrous, depending on the publication. In one of the trashier efforts, he found an article entitled "Shock Tactics." It was all about how to get the man of your choice. "Faint heart never won fair gentleman," he read. "Stun him. Invite him round and put on that naughty nightie and those sheer, sheer stockings." He put down the article, feeling slightly sad. There was something almost pathetic about Jane. It was as if she had so little self-esteem that she needed to find a personality in the pages of a magazine.

And then, on Christmas Eve, something happened that made him uneasy. He saw Jane slip a note into Diarmuid's hand. He wondered uneasily if Jane was after Diarmuid, and his heart sank. Jane was determined to seduce someone to get at John Wetherby. Did she realise that by getting at John she would have Heather to deal with? For if any affair was obvious enough for John to notice, then it would be plain as day to the horrible Heather as well.

He went to bed trying to work things out in his mind. There was a ferry arriving and leaving again on Boxing Day. He was determined to be on it. Jane needed a minder to protect her from malice, not a policeman, and she had enough money to hire one. He resolved to tell her that in the morning.

But he awoke very early, and in the distance he heard the reassuring sounds of domestic clatter. Then he remembered that Harriet was making the Christmas dinner, which was to be served in the middle of the day. He shaved and dressed and made his way to the kitchen. Harriet was bending over one oven, taking out a tray of mince pies. A huge stuffed turkey stood ready to be placed in the other, larger oven.

"My, you've been busy," said Hamish admiringly. She was wearing a scarlet wool dress and a frilly apron. Instead of her usual sensible walking shoes, she was wearing a pair of scarlet low-heeled pumps.

"My big day," said Harriet, avoiding his gaze. "Can I get you some coffee?"

"Yes, and you'd better tell me the truth about why you've been avoiding me," said Hamish. "Come on. If it's because I'm getting on your nerves, I'll float off like the Highland mist."

"No, it's not that," said Harriet slowly. She leaned her floury hands on the kitchen table. "I became a bit worried. I am not in a position to get into any emotional entanglements, and I like to cut them off before they start to happen. That's a bit muddled, but I'm sure you know what I mean. I began to sense something there. Attraction. On my side, at least."

Normally shrewd, Hamish should have asked her why she was avoiding any emotional entanglement, but he felt such a surge of elation that she found him attractive that common sense went out the window.

"Och, I'm not the type to get heavy," he said.

"There is also the question of age. I am forty-five and you, I judge, are somewhere in your early thirties."

"Is this a proposal of marriage?"

"Hamish Macbeth! Don't be silly."

"Well, then, I suggest we continue to be attracted to each other. Friends it is," said Hamish with a grin. "Need any help?"

She looked at him half-ruefully. "Yes, I could do with a bit of help. You do make me feel like a pompous fool. Friends we are. The oven's ready for the turkey, if you'd just put it in."

"Actually, I'm thinking of leaving on the ferry tomorrow," said Hamish after shutting the oven door. "It hasn't been the nicest of visits. Jane needs a minder, not a copper."

"I might leave with you," said Harriet, "although it will be a waste of left-over turkey."

"Why?"

"Jane doesn't really like the idea of meat. She'll probably throw the rest away. I won't be around to make turkey hash or turkey sandwiches."

"Then just wrap it up and I'll take it with me."

"Hamish Macbeth, whatever for?"

"It'll go to waste otherwise. She can't offer it to anyone on the island, her being so unpopular."

"All right, Hamish. If you are prepared to carry a turkey carcass back to Lochdubh, you are welcome."

"How did you come to write cookery books?" asked Hamish.

Harriet worked away at the kitchen table and told him about her writing career while pleasant smells filled the kitchen. The snow had disappeared, as it always seemed to do on Christmas Day, but there was the usual gale howling outside to intensify the air of cosiness inside.

After his pleasant morning, Hamish was prepared to find Christmas dinner a let-down—because of the nature of the guests rather than the cooking, which turned out to be superb. There was soup made from the turkey giblets, followed by the finest Scottish smoked salmon. Then came the turkey, brown and glistening, with chestnut stuffing and chipolata sausages. John carved the turkey and the atmosphere was fairly jolly. But it was Jane, not Heather, who turned things sour.

Sheila and Ian asked for second helpings and Hamish was just about to hand his plate over as well when Jane said seriously, "All this overeating is very bad for you, Sheila. Didn't I tell you in the summer that it was not crazy diets which took off the fat but sensible exercise and eating smaller meals?"

Sheila's face crumpled. "You're horrid," she said.

"What do you want my wife to look like?" demanded Ian furiously. "Some sort of girlish whore like you?"

Jane said in a maddeningly reasonable voice,

"Your affection and loyalty to your wife do you credit, Ian, but it is known as *enabling*, just like giving an alcoholic drink. I have often noticed..."

"Shut up, you stupid bitch," said John. "Don't you realise you are being downright *cruel?*"

Jane looked at him, open-mouthed.

"Here, now." Diarmuid leaped to Jane's defence. "It's Jane's job to see we are all healthy."

"Not while we're her guests," said Harriet. "Really, Jane, you are going to turn into one of those people who pride themselves on speaking their mind while they tramp over everyone's finer feelings."

Comforted by all the voices in her defence, Sheila took a plate of turkey from John, and then threw another metaphorical log on the already blazing fire. "Like Heather, you mean?" she said sweetly.

"Don't try and pick on me or it'll be the worse for you," said Heather. "I am glad I am a woman of independent mind and haven't got a brain stuffed with rubbish from romances."

"But you haven't got an independent mind, Heather dear." John brandished the carving knife at her. "It's full of Communist claptrap. You're the sort of woman who would have turned her husband and family over to the KGB, all to the glory of Joe Stalin. And furthermore, if you have such an independent mind, why do you try to dress like Jane?

She can get away with wearing short frocks because she's got good legs and a first-class figure while you just look like mutton dressed as lamb."

Harriet looked desperately at Hamish, who rose to his feet. He raised his glass. "Merry Christmas, everyone," said Hamish Macbeth.

Startled, they all muttered "Merry Christmas." Hamish remained on his feet.

"Her Majesty, the Queen," he proposed. All dutifully drank that one, except Heather. "And here's to our cook, Harriet Shaw," went on Hamish gleefully, while everyone hurriedly replenished their glasses. "*And* to our hostess."

Harriet began to giggle. "Do sit down, Hamish. You'll have us quite drunk."

But the sudden rush of alcohol into the systems of the angry guests worked well. The quarrels appeared to have been temporarily forgotten by the time the Christmas pudding was served.

After the meal was over, Jane led the party through to the lounge.

"Oh, dear," murmured Harriet, for under the tree was a pile of presents. Jane had bought presents for everyone. Harriet had guessed she would, but had forgotten to warn Hamish. Diarmuid got that item of headgear usually advertised in mail-order catalogues as a "genuine Greek fisherman's hat."

He was delighted and ran to a mirror to admire the effect. Harriet got a newfangled pastry-cutter; Sheila, a new romance called *Texas Heat;* Ian, a pair of slippers; John, a pocket calculator; Heather, a large volume entitled *The Degradation of the Working Classes in Victorian Scotland;* and there was even a present for Hamish. It was a grey-green sweater ornamented with strutting pheasants.

The guests then went to fetch their presents for Jane. "I forgot to warn you," whispered Harriet to Hamish. "Have you got anything?"

Hamish suddenly remembered the bottle of perfume in his luggage. He had bought it to give to Priscilla and had then forgotten about it, having packed it by mistake along with his shaving-kit. "I only need a bit of Christmas wrapping," he whispered.

Soon Jane was crowing with delight as she unwrapped her presents, although they were a singularly unimaginative set of offerings, from a cheque from her ex-husband to a record of protest songs from Heather.

"Gosh, I've eaten so much," sighed Heather.

"A good walk is what we need." Jane got to her feet. "Why don't you all go ahead and I'll catch up with you?"

Heather fumbled about the coats hanging at the doorway, complaining she could not find her oilskin. "Take mine," said Jane. "Save you time looking. I've got another one." So Heather put on Jane's yellow oilskin and all of them went out into the fierce gale.

It was after they had gone a mile along the beach that Hamish realised that Diarmuid and Heather were having a monumental row. The wind snatched their words away but then the little group saw Heather smack her husband's face. Diarmuid turned on his heel and strode back in the direction of the hotel. As he passed Hamish, his face was tense and excited.

Heather strode off inland, at right angles to the beach, without a word. The others huddled together and watched her go. "I wonder what all that was about?" said Sheila. "I thought they never had rows—well, hardly ever."

"Look," said Ian, "there's a truck coming along the beach."

Hamish recognised Geordie's antique Fiat. It drew to a stop beside them and Geordie jumped down. He held out his hand to Hamish. "I want tae thank you," he said. "I've neffer had a bit o' trouble wi' him since Macleod fixed things."

"There you are," said Hamish with a grin. "It's all in the mind. Where are you off to?"

"Skulag. I've had enough o' the missus. I'm going to the bar."

"Why don't we go with him?" Hamish asked the others. They all agreed, suddenly not wanting to go back to the health farm and spend the rest of Christmas Day with a warring Heather and Diarmuid.

"What about Jane?" asked John.

"I don't think she means to come," pointed out Hamish. "And besides, we never told her which way we were going on our walk."

"Two in the front and the rest up on the back," said Geordie.

They all rattled cheerfully on their way and were soon settled in the bar of The Highland Comfort, ignoring the hostile stares of the locals and getting quite tipsy. Geordie had said he didn't dare join them, lest the islanders damn him for consorting with "the enemy."

It was five o'clock when Hamish reluctantly suggested they should return. It had been so easy and companionable. The Carpenters had told stories of farming life in Yorkshire, John had related some very witty anecdotes about terrible judges, and Harriet had made them laugh with an account about being interviewed on television by an interviewer with a prepared list of questions who thought Harriet was a literary-prize winner and who had ploughed on regardless.

Geordie had disappeared, and so they all had to

walk back. Hamish took Harriet's hand. He knew he was quite drunk, a rare state of affairs for him. He felt warm and happy despite the howling wind and darkness. But as soon as he saw the pink sign of The Happy Wanderer, he experienced such a sharp feeling of dread that he let Harriet's hand drop and stood still.

"What's the matter?" asked Harriet.

He shivered. "Someone walking over my grave. Come on. Jane will be wondering what has happened to us all."

Jane and Diarmuid were seated in the lounge in front of the fire, side by side on the sofa. They rose to meet the company. Hamish looked at both of them sharply but Diarmuid looked much as usual, and Jane seemed delighted to see them, asking if they had enjoyed their walk.

"Where's Heather?" asked Hamish sharply.

"Still out. She walked off in a huff, if you remember," replied Diarmuid.

"She shouldnae be out in the dark on her own. She hadn't a torch." Hamish looked worried. "We're going to have to organize a search-party."

"It's not late," said Jane soothingly. "She's probably staying away to give us a fright."

"And she's succeeding wi' me," said Hamish grimly. He picked up a torch. "I'm going to look for her."

"I'm coming too," volunteered Harriet, not because she was worried about Heather but because she did not want to be with the others without Hamish.

"I think you ought to go too," said John, looking at Diarmuid with dislike. "That is, if you can tear yourself away from my wife."

"Ex-wife," said Diarmuid huffily. But he got to his feet and took his Barbour coat down from a hook at the door and then spent some time adjusting his new cap on his head. Not wanting to be left out of things, the Carpenters volunteered their services, and then Jane said she would go as well, for she knew the island better than any of them.

They split up outside. Harriet insisted on staying with Hamish and Sheila with her husband. Jane and Diarmuid and John looked at each other under the light of the pink sign and then, without a word, went their separate ways.

"I couldn't be on my own on an island like this," said Harriet, keeping close to Hamish. "It's spooky. You forget there are still parts of the world where there are no street lights, no shops, nothing but the howling wind and blackness."

For hours they struggled through endless miles of moorland and croftland, knocking at cottage doors from time to time, asking if anyone had seen Heather, but no one had.

It was nearly midnight when they returned, to learn from the others that Heather was still missing. Hamish went through to the phone and tried to rouse Sandy Ferguson, the policeman, but without success. He then phoned headquarters at Strathbane and ordered air-sea rescue patrols just in case Heather had been blown off some crag into the sea.

He sat up late while the others went to bed, waiting and hoping for Heather's return. In the morning, he set out at six and walked down to the village and began banging on doors and summoning all the men he could get to help in the search. Strangely, he knew there would be no difficulty. The islanders' spite did not extend to leaving some woman, possibly injured, lying out on the moors.

As dawn finally rose, he already had a line of men straggling out from the village, searching everywhere. The gale was tremendous, booming and shouting and roaring across the sky. Soon the brief daylight would begin to fade. Hamish looked up at the sky. There seemed little hope of any air rescue even getting off the landing strip in such weather.

Sandy Ferguson had sulkily joined the search. He looked more hung over than ever.

Hamish became aware that a red-haired child was studying him curiously as he searched around a large peat stack.

The boy crept closer. "Are ye looking for her?" he whispered.

"Aye," said Hamish. "A Mrs. Todd."

"I saw her sunbathing," said the boy.

Hamish looked at the white, pinched face and his eyes sharpened. "Could you take me to where she was sunbathing?"

"Aye, I could that, but it's ower on the west."

"What's your name, laddie?"

"Rory Sinclair."

Hamish called to one of the men on the road, who came running up. He drew him aside. "This boy's talking about seeing a woman sunbathing."

"Och, Rory's daft. A wee bitty simple."

"Still, we've got to try everything. You've got your car. Let's get the lad into it and get him to show us where he saw the woman."

Rory climbed into the passenger seat, highly excited at the thought of a trip in a car.

"Where on the west?" asked Hamish from the back seat.

"Balnador."

The car, an old battered Mini Cooper, chugged its way along roads which were little more than tracks, heading to the north-west of the island. "Vroom! Vroom!" said Rory, obviously enjoying himself hugely.

The car finally rolled to a stop. The driver said, "This is as far as I can get to the shore."

Hamish climbed out, helped Rory out of the front seat, and said, "Show me where you saw her."

The boy scampered ahead. The clouds parted and a fitful gleam of sunlight shone on the crags of rocks ahead, sticking up like broken teeth. The boy scrambled up them like a young deer, crouching before the wind. Then he shouted something that was torn away by the gale and pointed down.

Hamish scrambled up after him and lay on his stomach on a small triangle of mossy grass. The crag overlooked the sea. Huge waves were racing in, black and green and dashing themselves on a small pebbly beach. The thunder of the waves was deafening. The whole world seemed to be in motion. Waves reared up to tremendous heights before tumbling down with a powerful roar.

Hamish put his lips to the boy's ear.

"Where?"

Again the boy pointed down.

Hamish craned over the crag. And there down below, just beyond the fanning spread of the crashing waves, he saw a woman's foot.

Balancing against the ferocity of the wind, he turned and signalled to the driver, a small figure in the distance, and waited impatiently until the man crawled up to him. "She's here," bawled Hamish. "Get the doctor and get help, but take this lad away first."

When the boy had gone, Hamish slowly began to ease his way down to the small beach.

Heather Todd lay under a curve of overhanging rock. He stooped down and felt her pulse. Nothing. He examined her head and then gently lifted it. Her neck was broken and there was an ugly bruise on the side of it. He drew his knees up to his chin and waited, shivering, beside the dead body, for help to arrive.

Chapter Five

*I hope I shall never be deterred from detecting
what I think a cheat, by the menace of a ruffian.*

—Samuel Johnson

Hamish supposed there would be a doctor on the
island. There must be. He stood up and stretched
and looked up at the crag above him and then at
Heather's body. The only heights on the island were
the crags at various parts of the coast. How could
she have broken her neck? The crag was only about
fifteen feet above the beach. It was no enormous
cliff with a fall onto jagged rocks. Admittedly, if
she had bounced against one of the sharp projecting
edges, that might have done the trick.

The wind was less savage now and he could
clearly hear the sound of voices above him. Occasionally a torch beam searched him out as more
islanders began to gather. And then he heard Sandy

Ferguson's voice. "Is that you, Hamish? I'll send a couple of men down to collect her so that Dr. Queen can have a look at the body."

"No, you won't," shouted Hamish. "Nothing has to be touched. Get him down here and bring a tent to cover the body until the pathologist arrives."

There was the sound of swearing and then a scuffle followed by the clatter of falling debris as Sandy and a thin elderly man made their way down.

"This is Dr. Queen," said Sandy.

The doctor was a thin, spare man with a face set in lines of permanent arrogance. "I gather you're some sort of local bobby from the west coast," he said. "Well, stand aside, man, and let's have a look at her."

"Gently, now," warned Hamish. "Don't disturb anything."

The doctor ignored him. "Bring that lantern closer, Sandy," he said. "Mmm, yes. As I thought. She was blown off the top of the crag and broke her neck. Sad but straightforward. Get some men to take her up, Sandy, and get her put in my surgery while I prepare a report for the procurator fiscal."

"You are not to touch her." Hamish Macbeth stood foursquare beside the body.

"Why not?"

"Because I think it might be murder. I think someone struck her a savage blow on the neck wi' a rock."

"Dear me, don't be a fool, there's a good fellow," said the doctor.

"I repeat: no one touches this body until a team from Strathbane arrives," said Hamish stubbornly.

"You have not the authority. This is *my* island," protested Sandy.

"Aye, and you'll find yourself off it soon enough if I have my way," snapped Hamish. "I'm telling you to leave it where it is or, by God, I'll make trouble for both o' ye."

The doctor glared at him, but snobbery came to Hamish's rescue. Had Hamish been a holidaying policeman who was bird-watching or hiking, then Dr. Queen would have ignored him. But this Macbeth was a guest at The Happy Wanderer where, the doctor had learned, there was a barrister in residence. He and the other guests might back Hamish.

"Have it your way," he said haughtily. "But you're going to look a right idiot, wasting the taxpayers' money like this."

Hamish turned to Sandy. "Are you going to phone headquarters, or am I?"

"Oh, you do it, laddie," jeered Sandy.

"Then get a tent over the body and set two men to guard it. I'll be back."

One of the islanders ran Hamish to The Happy Wanderer. When he went into the lounge, the guests started up. There were also five of the island women there who, it turned out, worked as servants at the hotel during the season. Hatred for Jane seemed to have disappeared with the tragedy, and they were all exclaiming and commiserating in their soft island voices, changed from sinister threatening figures to a group of ordinary women.

"This is terrible," said Jane.

"Where is Diarmuid?"

"In his room. He's phoned his secretary, Jessie Maclean, and told her to get up here as fast as possible. I've heard of Jessie. Seems she does everything for him, including thinking, or that's the way Heather put it once."

"I've got calls to make," said Hamish, and Jane led him into the office and left him.

Hamish decided to phone the bane of his life, Detective Chief Inspector Blair, and make his report to him direct. If he did not, it was ten to one that it would be Blair who would arrive anyway, and a Blair sulky that Hamish had not told him about it firsthand.

Blair gave Hamish his customary greeting in his heavy Glasgow accent. "How are ye, pillock?"

"Listen," said Hamish. "I'm staying at a place called The Happy Wanderer on Eileencraig. One of the guests appears to have fallen off a crag and broken her neck, but I'm convinced it's murder."

There was a silence, and then Blair said sharply, "Are ye sure? Working in the holidays is a pain in the arse as it is, and ah'm no' that keen tae get the police helicopter oot on a wild-goose chase."

"I promised if there wass ever another murder, I'd let ye in on it," said Hamish. "I think you ought to come and bring the works."

"Oh, well, ah never cared much for Christmas anyways. As long as ah'm back for Hogmanay, it'll suit me. I could be daein' wi' the overtime."

Hamish briefly gave a description of where the body was to be found, what the local doctor had said, why he, Hamish, thought it might be murder, and a brief summary of the little he knew of the Todds. Blair recorded it all and told Hamish to watch the body and that he and the forensic team should be with him in a couple of hours.

Hamish rang off and then rested his elbows on the desk and wondered if he was making a fool of himself. The wind had been savage. She could easily have been blown off that crag.

The office door opened and Harriet came in and stood looking at him quietly. "Surely an accident," she said.

"It could be murder, Harriet."

"But we were all here!"

Not when we were searching for her, thought Hamish. Someone could have found her when they were out searching and struck her down.

"It's got to be investigated anyway," said Hamish wearily. "I've got to get back and make sure they don't move the body."

"Give me a few minutes and I'll come with you. I can make a thermos of coffee and some sandwiches and take blankets along. No, don't protest. It's better than waiting here. There are more islanders arriving, men this time. They're all being terribly nice to Jane. It's a great pity it had to be Heather's death that brought this about. I won't be very long."

Hamish went back to the lounge. Jane had found a long black dress and put it on. She was dispensing large whiskies to the islanders. Perhaps it was genuine sympathy, or perhaps because the news that free whisky being served acted on the Highland and Island brain wonderfully, but more islanders kept arriving every minute.

Hamish went to Diarmuid's room and quietly

opened the door. Diarmuid was sitting in an arm-chair, staring into space.

"I'll get matters cleared up as soon as possible," said Hamish quietly. "Are you all right?"

"My God," said Diarmuid in a low voice, "I don't feel a damn thing."

"Shock," said Hamish. "Do you want someone to sit with you?"

Diarmuid shuddered. "I'd rather be alone, Hamish."

"I'll send someone to fetch the doctor. You need a sedative to settle you for the night."

Hamish went back to the lounge. John Wetherby came up to him. "Can't you get rid of these people?" he asked. "This is hardly the occasion for a party."

"I think it's better for Jane that they stay," said Hamish. "It's high time they found out she's just an ordinary person like themselves."

John made a contemptuous noise which sounded like "garrr," and strode off. The Carpenters were talking to some of the islanders. They did not look shocked, rather they looked happy and excited. Ian was talking about sheep, a subject close to any islander's heart, and he had a rapt audience.

Harriet came back carrying a large bag. "Blankets and food," she said briskly.

"Right," said Hamish. "Now let's see if someone can lend me a car."

One islander, clutching a large tumbler of whisky, cheerfully parted with his car keys, and Hamish with Harriet made his way back over to the west.

The men put on guard were happy to be relieved. "We will chust be going over to that hotel to offer our condolences," said one eagerly.

"That's nice of them," said Harriet when the men had left after Hamish had instructed them to find Dr. Queen and send him to The Happy Wanderer to attend to Diarmuid.

"You'd be amazed if you knew how news travels up here," said Hamish. "They've got the wind of whisky. In another hour, an awf'y lot o' islanders will have found their way to The Happy Wanderer."

A small tent had been erected over Heather's body, much to Harriet's relief. The wind had dropped and the tide had started to go out. They sat down on the beach a little way away from the tent, wrapped in blankets, sipping hot coffee and eating turkey sandwiches.

"If it is murder," said Harriet suddenly, "have you taken into account that Heather was wearing Jane's oilskin?"

"Yes, I'd thought of that. But we all knew Heather was wearing it."

"But listen! The islanders didn't know, and Jane was wearing another of her yellow oilskins, an older

one, when we went out searching. In the dark, someone with a torch bent on murder might only see the
gleam of yellow."

"Could be. But I've a feeling, if it is murder, that
the intended victim was Heather."

"Wait a bit. Diarmuid could have staged that row.
Instead of going back to the hotel, he could have
followed Heather. It's always the husband, isn't it?"

"Yes, quite often," said Hamish slowly. "But keep
this to yourself. I thought Diarmuid had maybe
staged that row so as to go back and be alone with
Jane."

"I don't think that can be right." Harriet shivered and Hamish put an arm about her shoulders.
"Jane actually thought Diarmuid was a bit of a silly
ass. She said he had only married Heather for her
money because his real estate business was going
down the tubes. She rather liked Heather's adula-
tion for her. I can't really see Jane pinching anyone
else's husband."

"But I saw her slip him a note on Christmas Eve."

"Oh, well, you'll have to ask him about that. Let's
talk about something else. Tell me about your other
cases."

Hamish talked on and they sat huddled together
while the receding sea grew quieter.

Harriet was never to forget that night, sitting on

a lonely Hebridean beach with a constable's arm around her shoulders and a dead body only a few feet away.

And then after a long time had passed and both were getting sleepy, they heard the roar of helicopters. Hamish jumped to his feet and picked up the lantern and began to wave it. The forces of law and order from Strathbane had arrived.

HARRIET WATCHED, FASCINATED, for the next hour as photographs were taken and samples of pebbles and grit put into envelopes as a forensic team got to work. Detective Chief Inspector Blair and his sidekicks, Detectives Jimmy Anderson and Harry McNab, stood silent. Blair made a sour remark that Macbeth always seemed to have some female hanging about and retreated to the shelter of the helicopter which had brought him to the island and waited for the pathologist's report.

The pathologist eventually emerged from the tent. "Well?" demanded Hamish.

"Could be," he said laconically. "On the other hand, ten to one she broke her neck in the fall. The forensic boys are crawling over those rocks on the way down to see if they can find anything."

Blair's bulk appeared on the crag above their heads. "Is it murder?" he asked.

"Maybe," said the pathologist. "You can get the body photographed now. The forensic team'll probably be here the rest of the night and then I'll get the body flown over to the procurator fiscal in Strathbane."

Blair heaved a great sigh. "Come on up, Macbeth," he said. Blair was feeling thoroughly fed up. He wished he had not come. But Hamish had a gift for nosing out murders and Blair was frightened that, had he not come, the case might have been given to some young up-and-coming rival. Hamish and Harriet scrambled up after Harriet had neatly stowed blankets, thermos, and sandwich paper wrapping into the bag.

"Show us where this Happy Wanderer place is," said Blair. "We'll take the helicopter over. It's on the east, isn't it?"

Hamish nodded. He told one of the hovering islanders to take the car he had borrowed back to its owner. Harriet was tired. Everything was becoming unreal.

The helicopter lifted them over the island and landed on the beach in front of the health farm. It took a very short time, Eileencraig being only about thirty miles long and fifteen miles across at the widest part.

They all climbed down. Blair stood outraged.

All the lights in The Happy Wanderer were glaring out into the night. They could hear raucous "hoochs" and the sound of fiddle and accordion.

"Jings," said the pilot, sounding amused. "They've got a ceilidh on."

And sure enough, as Blair strode into the lounge, a full-scale party was in progress. Couples were dancing Scottish reels while the rest were clapping and shouting and cheering. Jane, face flushed, was enjoying herself, dancing a reel with a small bent man. The Carpenters were clapping in time to the music. There was no sign of either John or Diarmuid.

"Shut that bloody row!" bellowed Blair, his piggy eyes blazing with fury.

He stood blocking the doorway, a heavy-set figure of officialdom. The music stopped abruptly. As Blair, his detectives, Hamish, and Harriet walked into the room, the islanders slid past them and melted away silently into the night.

"Mrs. Wetherby?" demanded Blair, approaching Jane.

"Yes?"

"I am Detective Chief Inspector Blair from Strathbane. I am investigating the death of Heather Todd." With heavy sarcasm, he added, "I am right sorry to have broken up yer wee party."

"You mustn't be shocked, Mr. Blair," said Jane earnestly. "It's like a funeral, you see. People react to death in this way. It's shocking, but people are always jolly glad they're alive when anyone else has died. I read an article—"

"I'm no' interested in any article," glowered Blair. "Is there a room I can use for interviews? Ah'll need tae see the husband."

"I'm afraid that is not possible," said Jane firmly. "Dr. Queen has given him a sedative."

"Oh aye? Well, I'll start wi' the rest o' you. Macbeth, you can go tae yer bed. I'll let ye know if ye'r needed."

"That's not fair," protested Harriet. "It's his case."

"Neffer mind," said Hamish, although he was furious with Blair. "I need some sleep and so do you."

"Efter I've interviewed her," said Blair pompously, looking Harriet up and down.

Jane was efficiently clearing up dirty glasses and plates and stacking them on a tray. "You can use my office," she said, "but you had better let me know now how it is that the constable who found the body is being barred from the investigation."

Her upper-class accents fell unwelcomely on Blair's ears. Blair had made up his mind it was an accident and wanted to get back to the mainland as soon as possible, and he didn't want Hamish Macbeth around, throwing a spanner in the works. On the other hand, he didn't want to offend anyone who might raise a dust with headquarters. "I was merely concerned for his welfare," he growled. "All right then. You can stay, Macbeth. Show us to the office, Mrs. Wetherby, and we'll start with you."

Soon he was seated behind Jane's desk, with his detectives standing respectfully behind him. That was the way he liked it. Jane sat opposite and Hamish lounged over near the door and tried not to yawn.

"Now, Mrs. Wetherby...oh, we'd better have a copper take doon yer statement. Got yer notebook, Macbeth?"

"I'm on holiday," said Hamish patiently.

"All right, Anderson, you do it."

Jimmy Anderson found a hard chair in the corner and pulled out a notebook.

"I saw three policemen in the other helicopter," said Hamish, and Jimmy Anderson flashed him a grateful look.

"I'm no' going oot tae look for them," said Blair.

"Where is...the body?" asked Jane.

"At the doctor's surgery in the village," replied Blair. "Now, Mrs. Wetherby, let us begin."

It was then that Jane dropped her bombshell. "The murderer meant to kill me, not Heather."

Blair's eyes bulged. "Whit?"

So Jane told him all about the reason for Hamish's visit and about Heather's taking her coat and Blair groaned inwardly at this extra complication. Jane then went on to describe how the others had gone out for a walk. She had meant to follow them but had got a sudden headache and had taken a couple of aspirins and gone to bed.

Hamish looked at her suspiciously. He was sure Jane had never had a headache in her life, and furthermore would have been more apt to drink herb tea if she did have a headache, rather than take aspirin.

"And then I got up," Jane went on. The black dress had a deep V at the front. She leaned forward and stared at Blair, whose eyes goggled at the amount of rich cleavage exposed. "Diarmuid—Mr. Todd— was in the lounge and shortly afterwards I joined him. The rest, minus Heather, came back. We went out to search. I was on my own. I walked as far as the centre of the island before I gave up. I didn't see any of the other searchers until I got back."

Blair asked her a few more questions and then dismissed her after asking her to send John Wetherby in.

The barrister appeared looking cross, dressed in pyjamas and dressing-gown. He railed on for several minutes about the "indecent" party until he was silenced by Blair's remarking patronizingly that he had obviously never attended a Highland funeral, just as if he, Blair, had not been equally shocked by the festivities.

Blair's questions, to Hamish's surprise, were only perfunctory. His surprise increased as the Carpenters and Harriet were also questioned in the same brief manner. Where was Blair's usual hectoring and bullying?

They were finally all allowed to go to bed, Blair saying he would be back first thing in the morning.

"It nearly is morning," said Harriet to Hamish and then gave a cavernous yawn. "So much for a police grilling. He never really asked anything. Maybe he's saving his big guns for Diarmuid."

"Maybe," said Hamish, although in his heart of hearts he felt that Blair, who had worked Christmas so as to have extra time to enjoy the New Year celebrations, was only interested in getting it written off as an accident.

BLAIR DID NOT turn up until ten o'clock, and with him he brought Jessie Maclean, Diarmuid's secretary, who had arrived on a fishing boat. She was a slim, pale girl in her late twenties with straight brown hair and horn-rimmed spectacles.

Diarmuid was summoned to Jane's office. Jessie went to fetch him and tried to follow him in, but Blair told her sharply that as she had reported to him as soon as she had got off the boat and he had taken her statement, he had no more need of her.

Flanked by his detectives and this time with a uniformed policeman complete with tape recorder, Blair started his interrogation. Hamish hovered by the door, watching Diarmuid's bland and handsome face. He discovered to his surprise that he did not like Diarmuid, but why, he did not know. Heather had been so awful that all he had felt before for Diarmuid was mild pity.

"Now," said Blair, "we are sorry we have to put you through this, Mr. Todd, but I'll need your movements yesterday."

Diarmuid took out a pipe, filled it and lit it carefully. "I had a row with my wife when we were out walking, I confess that."

"What was it about?"

"Money," said Diarmuid. "I told her she would need to pull her horns in a bit when we got back to Glasgow. No more lavish entertaining. She took exception to this and stormed off. I walked about a bit and then returned to the hotel. There was no sign of Jane, so I read a book. Jane emerged from her room just as the others returned." He went on to describe the search, saying he had walked miles along the beach on the eastern side of the island in front of the hotel.

"I gather from Miss Maclean that your finances are in a bad way," said Blair.

"Well, I must admit the slump in house sales caused by the high interest rates caught me on the hop. That's why Heather and I could take such a long holiday. I dismissed the staff and locked up for the winter. I'd already sold off two of my branches, so there was just the main office left. What a mess. Thank God Jessie's here. She'll be able to sort it all out."

"Do you inherit anything on your wife's death?"

"Nothing but a joint overdraft," said Diarmuid.

"Was her life insured?"

Hamish listened hard.

"It was, but we didn't keep up the payments, so there's nothing from that." Diarmuid sighed heavily.

Blair looked at him sharply. "You know we can check on all this at the Glasgow end?"

"You don't even need to do that," said Diarmuid a trifle smugly. "Jessie's brought all the relevant business papers with her."

"Why should she do that?"

"Because I phoned her and told her to."

Blair looked at him suspiciously as he sat there smoking and frowning deeply, like an actor sitting smoking and frowning deeply. There was always something stagy about Diarmuid, Hamish thought.

The Detective Chief Inspector was worried. He did not like Diarmuid's attitude. He did not like the way he had had the foresight to get his secretary to come up, complete with papers. But Blair wanted to wrap the case up as soon as possible.

"How did Miss Maclean get here so quickly?" he asked.

"There's a night train from Glasgow to Oban, which arrives at six in the morning. I told her to get that and I phoned the hotel and arranged for one of the fishing boats to go over and pick her up."

"You must ha' paid a fair whack to get a fishing boat to go all that way."

"Yes, but I needed Jessie's help," said Diarmuid patiently.

"Who was the fisherman?" asked Hamish suddenly.

"Angus Macleod. Him that usually runs trips to the mainland for Jane," said Diarmuid.

"But," expostulated Hamish, "Angus Macleod iss the fellow who shut Jane up in that pillbox."

"What's this?" asked Blair.

With a studied patience that was beginning to get on Hamish's nerves, Diarmuid explained about the "prank." Hamish could almost sense Blair relaxing. There was now no doubt in Hamish's mind that Blair was going to do everything to prove Heather's death an accident, and unless Diarmuid was incredibly naïve, he was helping the inspector do just that.

Blair brought the interview to an end. He said he would go back to the hotel and see if the forensic team had reported in with anything.

Hamish went in search of Jane. "Would you mind very much if I stayed on for a bit?" he asked her. "I am convinced that Blair is going to drop the case. I would like to stay on and see if I can discover anything."

"Then you should," said Jane earnestly. "I can see you are dedicated to your job, Hamish, and you must have peace of mind or you will begin to suffer from *stress*."

Much as Hamish had expected, Blair came back in two hours' time and called them all together. "The forensic team found nothing on thae rocks or on the beach."

"Which proves," said Hamish quickly, "that someone must have struck her a blow on the neck. If she had hit a rock on her road down, then—"

"Aw, shut up," said Blair, his Glaswegian accent

becoming thicker in his irritation. "Better heads than yours, laddie, hiv discovered it was an accident. Mr. Todd, your wife's body has been taken to the procurator fiscal at Strathbane and can be recovered there. As I said, it was an accident, and that's that."

Hamish followed him out. "I don't think you really believe what you've just said," he remarked.

"Don't you tell me what I'm thinking or no' thinking," sneered Blair, "and remember you're addressing a senior officer. Accident, Macbeth. That's all. Anyway, you got a tasty piece there tae keep ye warm."

"Don't dare speak to me of Harriet Shaw in those terms," shouted Hamish.

"Ach, dinnae be daft. I'm no' speakin' about the auld bird what writes cookery books. Jane Wetherby. Yum, yum." And with a heavy wink, Blair got into a battered rented car. Jimmy Anderson, at the wheel, threw Hamish a sympathetic look before driving off.

Hamish went back indoors to hear Diarmuid say pathetically that he would like to stay on for a couple of days to recover before going to Strathbane to make arrangements for the body to be taken down to Glasgow for burial. Jessie, he said, was in the office making all the necessary phone calls.

Harriet looked at Hamish sympathetically. "Care to go out?" she asked.

Hamish looked at her, at her clear eyes, crisp hair and firm figure and felt all his anger and irritation melt away.

"What had ye in mind?" he asked.

"A late working lunch, copper. We've had nothing to eat. Get some paper and we'll go down to the hotel and try to work out who did it."

"So you think it might be murder as well?"

"Not exactly. But I think we ought to be sure. Blair's the sort of man who makes one want to prove him wrong."

They walked briskly towards Skulag. The day was crisp and clear, and for once, windless. The sea shone with a dull grey light on their left. Hamish was surprised not to see Geordie's truck. Geordie, it appeared, plied his way regularly between the west coast and the village of Skulag, bringing lobsters and fish over, to be loaded onto the ferry when it arrived for delivery to the mainland, or, in summer, put in a large refrigerator shed behind the jetty to await the arrival of the next ferry. In winter, it was always cold enough to store the seafood on the jetty. He also collected goods brought over by ferry or fishing boat and delivered them to various croft houses dotted over the island. He had been working over Christmas, so it was possible he had finally decided to take a rest. The islanders were mainly Presbyterian and a lot of them would think Christmas, despite its name, a pagan festival. Hogmanay—New Year's Eve—was the real celebration.

The owner of The Highland Comfort, who acted as barman and, it appeared, just about everything else, informed them sourly that the dining-room was closed in the winter but that they could have a meal in the bar. When they were seated, he handed them two greasy menus and left them to make up their minds.

"So much for Highland delicacies," mourned Harriet. "Chips with everything. Hamburger and chips, lasagne and chips, pie and chips, sausage and chips, and ham, egg and chips."

"I'll have the ham, egg and chips," said Hamish, "and a half pint of beer."

Harriet settled for the same. The landlord wrote their order down carefully. "I shouldnae hae tae do this mysel'," he complained. "But I cannae get staff. There wass wan girl left and herself walked out on me."

He slouched off.

"Since it'll probably take him about an hour to fry an egg," said Hamish, "let's get started." He opened out a folded pad of paper and took out a pen. "Jane Wetherby first. Any views?"

"I keep thinking about that coat," said Harriet eagerly. "Look, while Jane was away, we watched an Agatha Christie play on television. A woman calls in Poirot to protect her against somebody who has already tried to murder her. She invites her cousin to stay a few days with her. The cousin puts on the woman's highly coloured wrap and is killed by mistake. But it turned out that the cousin was the intended victim all along. The woman had manufactured attempts on her life to hide that fact. Jane wasn't with us. But she could have watched the show on television at her friend Priscilla's hotel."

Priscilla. Hamish looked startled. He hadn't phoned to wish anyone a happy Christmas. They would not know what he was up to, because there would only be about two lines in the newspapers describing the accidental death of a tourist on Eileencraig. Harriet was still talking.

"So you see, Hamish, we have something of the same scenario here. Jane told you of attempts on her life. And it was Jane who told Heather to take her coat. Jane could easily have lied about that headache and slipped out of the house by the back way. The question is... why?"

"That brings us to Diarmuid," said Hamish.

"Heather was older, a bore and a snob. He married her for her money and that money is gone. Did he have someone else ready to be Mrs. Todd Number Two? His business is so bad, he closed down for the whole of December and a bit of January. He could have run after Heather when he was out of sight of the rest of you, stalked her over to the west coast, waited until she climbed up on that crag, and then struck her on the side of the neck with a sharp rock. All he had to do then was hurl the rock in the sea. As I told you, I saw Jane slipping him a note. Jane is a very wealthy woman with a good business. She's also got looks, and Heather had none. Worth killing for, don't you think? Diarmuid is incredibly vain, and vain men are dangerous."

"What about John Wetherby?" asked Harriet. "You know, Hamish, for all his sour manner, I think he's still in love with Jane. What if something made him go mad with jealousy? What if he went over the edge and struck down Heather when we were searching for her, seeing only that yellow oilskin and thinking it was Jane?"

Hamish wrote busily. "We'd better check into John Wetherby's business affairs and find out if Jane still has a will in his favour, that is, if she ever had one. What about the Carpenters? Is there something there?"

"I don't think so," said Harriet roundly, "and neither do you. But I suppose they'll have to be checked into as well. But how can you do it, not being officially on the case?"

"Wonder o' wonders," said Hamish, "here comes our food and beer."

As they munched their way through greasy chips, salty, fatty ham and watery eggs, and drank their flat beer, Hamish kept looking down at his notes. "I think I should find out what was in that note Jane slipped to Diarmuid," he said. "But then, we should concentrate more on Heather's character. See what you can get out of that secretary. Make a friend of her."

Harriet grinned. "Right you are, Sherlock."

WHEN THEY RETURNED to the health farm, it was to find Diarmuid had retreated to his room again. The rest, including Jessie, were watching television.

Harriet asked Jessie if she would like to take a walk and get a bit of fresh air. Jessie agreed and the pair walked outside.

Harriet studied her companion as they both strolled along the beach. Jessie was attired in a chain store's contribution to "power dressing." She had on a pin-striped suit, the jacket having very large square shoulder pads, and a short tailored skirt. With it, she wore a high-necked white blouse and black court shoes with low heels.

After some general conversation on the tragedy, Harriet asked curiously, "But what about you? What will you do now? I mean, I gather Diarmuid's business was pretty much finished."

"Oh, there'll be a lot of winding-up of affairs," said Jessie. "I'll be kept busy. Then I might go away somewhere. Try going to another country."

"But you've had a month off."

"And glad of it, too," said Jessie waspishly. "The Todds were a couple of slave-drivers."

"How can that be, if the business wasn't doing at all well? I mean, what was there to do?"

Jessie stopped and looked at Harriet suspiciously and then shrugged. "It was her that was the problem. I don't believe that woman even knew how to wipe her own backside." The crudity sounded odd, spoken as it was in Jessie's prim, Scottish-accented, carefully elocuted vowels. "Who do you think did all the work, setting up her 'little parties'? Who typed her damn letters to this and that? Me. Even if the business hadn't collapsed, I meant to leave anyway."

"Did she entertain much?" Harriet watched Jessie closely, thinking what a moody, rather spiteful girl she appeared.

"Oh, lots. It was all supposed to help the business. Invite the 'right' people in the hope they would become clients, lavish drink and concert tickets on them. And a useless lot they were, too. Occasionally she'd net a celebrity, by playing one celebrity off against the other, you know—'Mr. Bloggs is coming, Mr. Biggs,' and Mr. Biggs is reassured that there is to be another eminent celebrity, as is Mr. Bloggs when he is phoned and told that Mr. Biggs is coming. Old trick, but a surprising lot fell for it. I think Mr. Todd will find he hasn't a friend in the world when it gets about he hasn't any money." This was said with a peculiar relish.

"Heather told me some very colourful stories about her upbringing in the Gorbals when it was one of the worst slums in Glasgow," said Harriet, "so how did she have so much money?"

Jessie sniffed. "That was one of her lies to make her a genuine member of the left. She was brought up as an only child in a large house in Hillhead, which, in case you don't know, is a posh suburb near the university. She became left-wing to get an entrée into a society which would otherwise have rejected her— you know, theatre, writing, the arts."

"Was Diarmuid a good boss?"

"Yes, he'd have been all right on his own, but he expected me to work for his wife as well."

"So why didn't you leave? How long were you with them?"

"Six years. Look, they paid well, I'll say that for them. I've always wanted to live in Spain and I've kept that as my goal. Now, I'm cold. Run off and tell that copper boy-friend of yours everything I've said because that's the only reason you're marching me along this cold beach."

And Harriet Shaw had the grace to blush.

Chapter Six

...the motive-hunting of motiveless malignity—
how awful it is!

—Samuel Taylor Coleridge

Hamish returned to the village alone and ran Angus Macleod to earth. After lecturing the unrepentant fisherman on his disgraceful behaviour, pushing Jane into the pillbox, Hamish asked him about that phone call from Diarmuid, requesting him to pick Jessie up at Oban.

"Oh, aye, he phoned in the middle o' the evening in a rare state," said Angus. "Asked me to take the boat out and go tae Oban. I telt him tae get lost, but he offered me a lot and the wind was dying, so ower I went."

"Had you ever seen the girl, Jessie Maclean, before?"

"No, first time I'd seen her."

Hamish then took himself along the main street to Mrs. Bannerman's cottage. She was furious when he questioned her about her movements on the night of the murder, but eventually said she had been at a neighbour's party. Hamish checked with the neighbour, a Mrs. Gillespie, who confirmed that Mrs. Bannerman had been there all evening. But the murder could have been committed earlier, thought Hamish. No pathologist could ever tell the exact time of any murder. The closest he could come to it was between about four in the afternoon and nine in the evening. Hamish asked Mrs. Gillespie if she had seen Mrs. Bannerman earlier and got the reply that Mrs. Bannerman had also been there in the late afternoon, helping Mrs. Gillespie with the arrangements for the party.

By the time Hamish returned to The Happy Wanderer, he was beginning to wonder whether Heather had actually fallen to her death after all. There did not seem to be any motive. He was told Diarmuid was still in his room. When Hamish opened the door, Diarmuid was lying flat on the bed, looking at the ceiling.

"I just want to ask you one thing," said Hamish. "On Christmas Eve, Jane slipped you a note. What was that about?"

Diarmuid struggled up and smoothed down his

ruffled hair with a careful hand, looking across at himself in the mirror. "Oh, that? I asked her if she had any contacts in the real estate business. I'm looking for a buyer. She gave me a note telling me to try James Baxter of Baxter, Fredericks and Baxter. James Baxter is an old acquaintance of hers. She bought the health farm from him. He's expanding his business."

"I don't suppose you kept the note," said Hamish suspiciously.

"Of course I did," said Diarmuid crossly. He got up and went to the dressing-table and slid open one of the drawers. "Here it is. I meant to give it to Jessie so that she could make an appointment for me to meet Baxter when we got back to Glasgow."

"I'll just take this for a while," said Hamish.

"Don't you think I have enough to bear?" demanded Diarmuid with a rare show of animation. "Good God, man, my wife's *dead!* It's an *accident.* Jessie says, and quite rightly, that you have no authority."

"I'll hae a word wi' the lassie," said Hamish grimly. "But I'll be keeping this note for now." He turned in the doorway. "By the way, where was your wife's coat, the one she couldn't find?"

"Hanging in the wardrobe," said Diarmuid. "Over there. The police examined it but could find nothing sinister about it."

Hamish ran Jane to earth in the kitchen. "I want to ask you about Diarmuid," he said. Jane turned a little pink and stirred something she was cooking energetically. "What?"

"This note." Hamish held it out. "Did you write it?"

Jane glanced at it. He sensed she was relieved and wondered why. "Yes, it's the name of a big estate agent," she said. "He wants to sell what's left of his business."

Hamish thanked her, returned the note to Diarmuid, and went back to the lounge, where Harriet drew him aside and repeated the conversation she had had with Jessie. "Are you sure it isn't just an act?" asked Hamish. "I mean, she's a wee bitch in my opinion, but there's something, well—sexy—about her. Don't you think she and Diarmuid...?"

"Nothing there that I can see except a lot of contempt for her employer on Jessie's side," replied Harriet. "How did you get on?"

Hamish told her in a low voice the result of his investigations while John Wetherby, reading a London newspaper that had come over on the Boxing Day ferry and had been delivered along with other newspapers and magazines, suddenly glared at them suspiciously over the top of it.

"I would like to think there might have been

some sort of collusion between Jessie and Diarmuid," Hamish said. "That contemptuous manner
of hers could be all an act."

"But she wasn't even on the island," pointed out
Harriet.

"Nonetheless, there could be something between
them, and if there is, they'll drop their guard pretty
soon. I cannae stand that Diarmuid. His vanity is
pathological."

"Are you sure you are not letting this dislike of
Diarmuid colour your attitude?" asked Harriet.

Hamish laughed. "I'll try not to. Where's Jessie?"

"Watching television."

Hamish went into the television room. Jessie
was sitting with the Carpenters. Hamish looked
thoughtfully at the Carpenters. Was he right to dis-
miss them so easily as possible suspects? But he
leaned over Jessie and said quietly, "A word with
you, Miss Maclean, if you please."

She followed him out. "We'll use Jane's office,"
said Hamish.

"I asked Jane about you," said Jessie when they
were seated on either side of the desk. "You're nothing but a bobby from some hick Highland village,
and you have no right to bother my employer or me
with questions. It was an accident."

"Then if it was only an accident, you should not

object to my questions," said Hamish mildly. "I thought Diarmuid was your ex-boss anyway."

"I'm working for him until the funeral arrangements are over and I've promised him I'll pack up Heather's effects."

"And then what?" asked Hamish.

She shrugged her thin shoulders. "Probably go abroad for a bit."

"Where?"

"Spain, somewhere like that."

"Did Diarmuid ever have extra-marital affairs?" Her reply startled him. "Lots."

"And did Heather know about any of them?"

Again that shrug. "I suppose she did. He's not good at keeping anything quiet."

"Neither was she," said Hamish drily. "She must have given him a rare blasting."

"Not she. She didn't mind what he did as long as he toed the line and paid out for all the entertainment for her parties and bridge clubs and golf clubs and what not. She wasn't interested in sex. He tried to tell her the money was running out due to the housing slump. I tried as well. But she wouldn't listen. She couldn't imagine a life where she wouldn't be lording it at one of her get-togethers and fancying herself as a leader of Glasgow society. This year was the worst."

"Why?"

"Well, Glasgow got the award of Cultural Capital of Europe, and that meant more celebrities to try to get into her home."

"Have you ever had an affair with him?"

"Don't be daft," said Jessie. "The man's useless. All he's ever really fancied in the whole of his life is his own reflection."

Hamish told her that would be all for the moment, and once on his own, thought about her. He thought she was as hard as nails. Had she been Diarmuid's Lady Macbeth?

After dinner, he tried to question John Wetherby, but John told him acidly that he had no right to question anyone.

Hamish retreated once more to the office and phoned Detective Jimmy Anderson in Strathbane. "You're lucky," said Jimmy. "Blair's off on holiday. Never tell me it's murder or he'll be having your guts for garters."

"I'm trying to find out," said Hamish. "That John Wetherby. I was wondering if he's such a successful barrister after all."

"Believe me," said Jimmy with a laugh, "Blair checked into everyone when he returned, just to make sure. I'll get out the file if you want to hear it."

Hamish readily agreed.

After a few moments, Jimmy came back on the line. "Here we are. Wetherby, John. Yes, rolling in money. Got family money as well as earned money. Very successful.

"Carpenters. There's a surprise. Now they're *rich*. Own a good part of north Yorkshire. Told friends they were looking forward to a free holiday. Like all rich people, they seem to love getting something free.

"Jane Wetherby. Good family. Not all that much money. Made a success out o' that health farm o' hers. Got a reputation of being a loose woman." Hamish grinned: nothing like the Scottish police for using old-fashioned terms. If Jimmy had called her a harlot, it wouldn't have been surprising either. "Not much known about her. Seems to have hundreds of dear acquaintances and not a single friend. Got a younger sister, Cheryl, who says Jane's bats.

"Harriet Shaw. Successful writer. Talks on cookery on television and radio. Moderately well off. Knew Jane slightly, I gather. Widowed.

"Diarmuid. Well, we really dug into him. Business on the skids but nothing to gain from his wife's death. Few affairs on the side but no grand passion."

"What about the secretary, Jessie?" asked Hamish.

"She turned up on the island *after* the death.

But she's been employed by him for six years. One of the office staff said she ran the business, not Diarmuid."

"So why did it become so unsuccessful? Jessie?"

"Naw. There's estate agents closing down all over the place."

"Well, thanks, Jimmy; I'm only surprised Blair went to so much trouble."

"Blair! It was me he got to go to the trouble, Hamish. He's that frightened you'll spring a murder on him and make him look a fool."

Hamish thanked him and rang off. He sat chewing the end of a pencil, thinking over the case. Why? Why had anyone wanted to murder Heather? She had been a nasty woman. But there was no motive. Diarmuid did not stand to get any money from her death. Why?

He decided to stay awake that night, to wait and watch and see if anyone else also stayed awake. If, say, Jessie and Diarmuid were involved, then they would be desperate to speak to each other.

He waited until they had all gone to bed and then went into the lounge and sat down in the darkness. The hours passed slowly. There was still no wind outside and the silence was eerie.

And then, at two in the morning, just as he thought he could not keep his eyes open any longer, the light in the corridor leading to the bedrooms went on.

Hamish rose silently and crossed to the window and hid behind the curtains. He peered through the thick folds.

Jane came in, followed by Diarmuid. "What is it, darling?" asked Diarmuid. "What's happened?"

"I'm worried," said Jane in a low voice. "That secretary of yours is very much in your confidence. You must not ever tell anyone what we did."

"Are you mad?" demanded Diarmuid. "Get rid of that tame copper of yours, for God's sake."

"There's a ferry the day after tomorrow," said Jane. "Believe me, you'll all be on it."

"But the ferry left on Boxing Day. There won't be another for a week. I was going to hire Angus to take me across."

"This is an Oban company. It's a small ferry which doesn't take cars, only passengers. I suggest you and Jessie get on it. You can hire a car in Oban and get from there to Strathbane."

Diarmuid shivered. "I'll send Jessie. I couldn't bear to see Heather's face again."

"That's understandable. Now get off to bed, Diarmuid, and let me get to mine. I'm tired."

He stretched out his arms. "Jane..."

"Oh, leave me alone," said Jane crossly.

Hamish waited until all was quiet and went to Harriet's room and walked in. He woke her up and then switched on the bedside light and sat on the edge of her bed.

"What is it?" demanded Harriet.

"I hid in the lounge and heard Diarmuid and Jane talking." Hamish told her what they had said. "So it's plain to me they arranged this murder between them."

"No, Hamish," said Harriet. "Look, Jane would never be involved in any murder. I've changed my mind about her. She couldn't hurt a fly."

"Oh, no? What do any of us really know about Jane? Everyone here only knows her slightly. Diarmuid's had affairs before because Jessie told me. But just think. Jane is now rich. She's attractive. Without Heather around, he can marry her."

"But you have no proof," wailed Harriet. "An overheard conversation is no proof. What are you going to do?"

"Shock tactics," said Hamish. "Just wait and see."

HAMISH WAITED UNTIL they were all gathered in the lounge after breakfast and then stood in front of the fire facing them.

"I think I have discovered why the murder of Heather Todd was committed," he said.

There was a long silence and then a babble of outraged voices. "It was an accident," snapped Jane. "You insensitive, posturing clod," commented John Wetherby. "Really!" screamed the Carpenters.

Hamish held up his hands for silence. "Hear me out," he said.

"The murder was committed by Jane Wetherby and Diarmuid Todd." They gazed at him open-mouthed.

"It was all planned," said Hamish. "All they needed was the opportunity. The stage had been set by having so-called attempts on Jane's life. I was invited over to make everything more realistic. With everyone going for a walk on a wild day, Jane suggested that Heather take *her* coat so that she could claim, as she later did, that she, Jane, had been the intended victim, not Heather. Either Diarmuid followed Heather and murdered her, or he returned to the hotel and collected Jane and they murdered her together."

Jane burst into tears and Diarmuid slowly rose to his feet, ashen-faced.

The others sat around stricken.

"I am afraid I hid in the lounge last night and listened to your conversation," said Hamish. "I heard you, Jane, tell Diarmuid that no one must ever know what you had done." He looked steadily at the weeping Jane.

Then Jane straightened and marched up to Hamish, proud bosoms jutting, head thrown back. "I know how it must look," she said, "but you see..." She swung round and shouted at Diarmuid, "For goodness' sake, *tell* him! Do you want to be tried for murder?"

Diarmuid just stood there, looking miserable.

Hamish had an awful feeling that his beautiful love-triangle-murder theory was falling into ruins somewhere in his head. "You tell me," he said to Jane.

Jane said loudly, "We couldn't have done it. Either of us. *We were in bed together.* I was lonely. I needed someone. Then Diarmuid came back. He needed someone, too. He was dejected because his business had collapsed and Heather was treating him like dirt because he couldn't finance her little salons any longer. We had just got dressed and were back in the lounge when you all came back. Don't you see, that's what I meant when I said no one must ever know." She rounded on John Wetherby. "You're sitting there smirking; well, hear this! This was the first affair I've had in years. I was never unfaithful to you. I only pretended to be to get revenge for your insults and slights and nasty remarks. And all that's happened is that I've been to bed with some useless geek. I hate men!

"So did we bash Heather while pretending to look for her? No, we did not, for I wouldn't go anywhere with Diarmuid, not ever again."

John Wetherby came to her side and put an arm about her waist. "I'll sue this copper for harassment, Jane."

"Piss off, all of you," shouted Jane, her face contorted with rage. "There's a ferry leaves tomorrow. Be on it. All of you!"

She stormed out.

Hamish stood silent, feeling like an utter fool. How could he have ever suspected Jane? Harriet had been right. It was his dislike of Diarmuid that had coloured his judgement.

Jane's voice had held the ring of truth.

"Let's get out of here." It was Harriet at his elbow.

Sadly Hamish trailed out after her. The tide was out and they walked side by side over the hard white sand towards the sea. The sand was covered at low tide by an inch of water and the flat island soon disappeared behind them, leaving them walking across a mirror of water. Large clouds sailed overhead and under their feet. The absence of any feeling of land or place gave Harriet a slight feeling of vertigo. They came to a stop and stood together.

"How weird this is," said Harriet softly. "Standing in the middle of nowhere. In the cities there are lights and people and noise. No wonder poor Geordie is mad. I would go mad myself if I lived on this island for very long."

"I think it hass affected my wits." The sibilancy of Hamish's accent showed how distressed he was. He hadn't even phoned Priscilla, he had been so hell-bent on finding a murderer. Let it go, his mind told him, it was an accident. Let it go.

"Let's go down to Skulag," said Harriet.

They walked back together. A wind sprang up and began to ruffle the surface of the water beneath their feet. They had reached the road and had gone a little way along it when an islander stopped his car beside them and offered them a lift. They gratefully accepted, remorseful Hamish glad of this sign of the islanders' new tolerance for Jane; before Heather's death, no one would have stopped to offer any guest from The Happy Wanderer a lift.

But to his fury, when they reached The Highland Comfort, the driver stretched out a dirty paw and said, "That'll be twa pund and fifty pee."

"Two pounds and fifty pence for what?" demanded Hamish.

"That's whit ye'd pay for a taxi," said the driver.

Harriet turned away as the normally mild Hamish Macbeth told the driver what to do with his car and where to put it before joining her in front of the hotel.

"That was all I needed," said Hamish angrily.

"Whisky's what we need," said Harriet bracingly. "I can't drink any more of that gnat's piss they call beer."

When they were seated by the window in the bar, each nursing a large glass of whisky, Harriet looked at gloomy Hamish and said gently, "You mustn't give up now. You were so sure it was murder."

"Aye, but I'm right sorry about Jane. I cannae bring to mind a time before when I made such a fool of myself."

"It's the motive that's lacking," said Harriet.

Hamish looked at her. "The motive usually lies in the person themselves. That is, the murderee. What are the usual motives? Passion and money, but usually money. Of course, there's drink or drugs, but I think whoever it was put an end to Heather had all their wits about them. I cannae think what else I can do. I am sure that the clue to the whole business lies somewhere in Glasglow. Talk to me about Heather."

"There's nothing more than I've already told you." Harriet looked out at the jetty. Geordie's truck was parked there, and as she watched, the small figure of Geordie came round the side of it and gave the truck a savage kick in the tyre. "Geordie's just kicked his truck," said Harriet. "He shouldn't have done that."

"You're getting as bad as him." Hamish cast an indifferent glance out of the window. "Go on about Heather."

"Let me see. Oh, I know." Harriet's face lit up. "You'll never believe this, but I came across her reading that romance of Sheila's. She was so absorbed in it, she didn't even notice me."

"So much for her hating romances," commented Hamish.

"She seemed to have an obsession about them," said Harriet. "She cornered me and asked me to go for a walk with her, and then, as soon as we were walking along the beach, she started to grill me about how much romance writers made. I said there were romance writers and *romance writers,* you know, from the trash to the really top-level stuff. First-time authors in Britain often get as little as two hundred pounds a book. She said—let me think— she said that surely America was the market. What about New York publishers? I said I thought it was possible for a first-time author to get a lot of money, provided the book was a block-buster. I got the strange impression she had written one, but when I asked her, she denied it with her usual sneers."

"We've got nothing else to go on." Hamish sat and thought hard. "Look, do you have a New York agent?"

"Yes, and a very good one."

"Would he know if there was a block-buster in the offing, say, one with a background of Glasgow? What else do we know about Heather? She claimed to have been brought up in the Gorbals, that horrible slum, or it was when she was growing up. See if there's any hint of a book. It's a bit far-fetched. But if Heather had actually pulled it off and was due a large sum of money, which her husband would inherit, then Diarmuid might find it worthwhile to push her off that crag after breaking her neck."

"So back to Diarmuid. Are you sure...?"

"No, I am not letting my dislike colour my judgement this time. Could you phone your agent?"

"All right," said Harriet. "So long as Jane gives me permission."

When they arrived back at The Happy Wanderer, it was to find the place wearing an air of mourning caused more by Jane's desire to get rid of her guests than by Heather's death. It was a new Jane, tight-faced and brisk. She snapped at Harriet that, yes, she could use the phone in the office provided she paid for the call.

Hamish waited anxiously in the deserted lounge. The other guests were hiding in their rooms, either to pack, but mostly, he guessed, to keep out of Jane's way.

Harriet emerged from the office, her face shining. "Where can we talk?"

"Television room," said Hamish. "I don't think there's anyone in there."

They walked in together. For once the television set was silent. "My agent says there's a block-buster all right, but he doesn't know who it's from or what it's worth, or what it's about. But it might just have a Scottish background. He says he'll ask around. I've to phone back in a couple of hours." Elated, Harriet gave Hamish a kiss, but he was too absorbed in this new information to take much notice of it.

The next two hours seemed to drag past. They sat and watched a rerun of a Lassie movie without either of them seeing much of it. Then Harriet rose and went to phone her agent again.

"Come with me, Hamish," she said. "Let's see what he has found out."

Hamish waited, tense, while she spoke to her agent again. Finally she put down the phone and took a deep breath. "Oh, Hamish, he found out the publisher and editor responsible for this book, but in fairness he cannot be expected to be told the details of a book not yet published. But—get this! The word is that the advance was half a million dollars!"

Hamish performed a mad, erratic sort of Highland

fling round the room while Harriet called the New York publisher and got through to the editor who was handling the book. Hamish stopped his cavorting and listened. He quickly gathered that the editor was amazed that a stranger should ask such questions about an unpublished book. He grabbed the phone and introduced himself. "I am a policeman investigating a death in Scotland," he said. "The name of the dead woman is Heather Todd. Is that, by any chance, the name of the author?"

"No," said the editor reluctantly. "I can at least tell you that much. Heather Todd is not the name of the author." Hamish thanked her nonetheless, and said he would be most grateful if he could call again. She agreed and he sadly put down the phone.

"Damn," he said. "I'm now sure there's something there. Damn. If only I could get to Glasgow."

"We're leaving tomorrow. We could go together," said Harriet eagerly.

"I'll need to find out if one of my relatives can put me up," said Hamish cautiously. "My mother's from Glasgow."

"Be my guest," said Harriet. "I'll get us both hotel rooms."

"But hotels are awf'y expensive," protested Hamish.

"Don't worry. I'm enjoying this. Say yes, Hamish.

You wouldn't want the murderer to get away with it, now would you?"

"All right." Hamish capitulated. "If you're sure."

THE GUESTS ASSEMBLED on the wind-swept jetty at dawn the following day. "Going to be a rough crossing," volunteered John Wetherby, practically the first words he had said to anyone since Jane's outburst. Jane had run them all to the jetty in relays and had left without saying goodbye to any of them.

Hamish saw Angus Macleod walking up the jetty and went to meet him. "I've been thinking," said Hamish, "when you went to get Jessie Maclean, was there any other passenger?"

"No, only herself," said Angus.

"I don't suppose you do these passenger trips often. I mean, the islanders will usually wait for the ferry."

"Aye, that's right. The only private passenger I've had was that sulky bitch o' a maid from the hotel."

"When was that?" asked Hamish sharply.

"Och, when I wass going to pick up that Jessie female at Oban. The maid heard I wass going and asked me to take her across."

"What did she look like?"

"Red hair and a fat face."

Hamish walked back to join Harriet. "Do you

remember the first time we went to the bar in Sku-lag?" he asked.

Harriet nodded.

"Do you remember that maid at the hotel? She was just about to come down the stairs when she saw us and darted back."

"Yes, I remember."

"Get a good look at her?"

"Good enough. She was fat with red hair. Why?"

"I thought I was on to something for a moment. When Angus went over to pick up Jessie, he took that maid across to Oban. I was hoping for a moment it might have been Jessie herself, trying to fool us."

"But it couldn't have been Jessie, even a Jessie in disguise," said Harriet.

"Why?"

"Because immediately after Heather was found dead, Diarmuid phoned Jessie in *Glasgow*."

"Aye, I'm grasping at straws. Here comes the ferry." Hamish pointed out to sea, where a small boat was bucketing through the waves.

"And here comes Jane," cried Harriet.

The jeep drove onto the jetty and Jane climbed out. She was wearing a pair of jeans which looked as if they had been painted on, high-heeled sandals, and a low-necked blouse worn under a short blue jacket.

She approached the shivering group with hands outstretched. "My dear friends," she cried, "I could not possibly let you go like this. I have been in communion with my inner being and found peace. I do not bear any resentments, even to you, Hamish Macbeth. Let us all shake hands and part friends."

Only John Wetherby made a sound of disgust. Sheila hugged Jane to her maternal bosom and thanked her for her hospitality with tears in her eyes. Diarmuid shook hands with Jane but did not raise his eyes to her face. Jessie gave her a firm handshake and the rest followed suit.

"I'll stay if you like," said John Wetherby harshly.

"I'll be all right," said Jane, the smile of rather fixed serenity she was wearing fading, to be replaced by a puzzled look. "Why?"

"I've got two more weeks' leave and I can't stand the idea of you being here on your own."

"All right then," said Jane, a genuine smile illuminating her face.

"Oh, dear," said Hamish, watching the odd couple walk off together to the jeep. "I hope I'm not barking up the wrong tree."

The ferry bumped against the jetty and bucketed up and down as they walked on board, carrying their luggage. Hamish and Harriet stood side by side at the rail, watching fish and lobsters being loaded on. "Where's Geordie with his load, I wonder?" said Hamish.

"Here he comes." Harriet pointed. The Fiat truck was racing down the village street. It hurtled onto the jetty. They could see Geordie's face behind the wheel contorted with fear.

The truck kept on going, plunged over the corner of the jetty, missing the end of the ferry, and sank into the sea like a stone.

Hamish ran down the gangplank, tearing off his coat as he went. He was about to plunge into the sea when Geordie's head appeared above the waters, bobbing like a cork. He swam to the iron ladder at the side and crawled up it, dragged the final few rungs by helping hands.

"What happened?" demanded Hamish.

"He tried tae kill me," said Geordie. "But I got the better o' him. Himself's dead now."

"Was your truck insured?" asked Hamish.

"Tae the hilt, man," panted Geordie. "Tae the hilt. I'll hae a bran'-new beastie soon enough."

Hamish darted back to the ferry and ran on board, picking up his coat on the way.

The gangplank was pulled up, the ropes released, and the ferry chugged out to sea.

"He shouldn't have kicked it," mourned Harriet.

"Havers," said Hamish bitterly. "That brother o' Angus's tricked me and did a shoddy job."

But Harriet said nothing. She leaned on the rail and watched until the small figures gesticulating around Geordie slowly disappeared from view.

Chapter Seven

Vanity, like murder, will out.

—Hannah Cowley

Glasgow. Hamish was bewildered.

He had not visited the city in years. Everything seemed to have changed. Landmarks he had known as a child were gone forever. What of St. Enoch Square, which was once commanded by the station hotel, the very epitome of Victorian architecture? All gone, down to the tin advertisement which used to be on the wall opposite the Renfrew bus stop: "They Come As a Boon and a Blessing to Men, The Pickwick, the Owl, and the Waverley Pen." Now there was a large glass pyramid, very much like the one outside the Louvre in Paris, but housing a shopping centre covering the whole area of the square.

He and Harriet had left their bags in a small hotel in the Great Western Road and had taken a taxi to drive them about the city. They dined in an Italian restaurant after their tour, Harriet saying they should have an early night and start their investigations in the morning. Diarmuid had hired a car in Oban and had gone, after all, with Jessie to Strathbane to make arrangements for Heather's body to be taken south to a funeral parlour in Glasgow.

Hamish said good night to Harriet outside her hotel room. All of a sudden he found himself remembering that impulsive kiss she had given him and wondering if he could have another. But by that time, she had closed the door. He was strongly attracted to her, that he realised, and then, hard on that thought, he remembered Priscilla. He went to his own room and dialled the Tommel Castle Hotel.

To his amazement, he was told Priscilla was not back yet. He asked for Mr. Johnson and soon the hotel manager of the Lochdubh Hotel was on the line. "How're you getting on?" asked Hamish.

"Just fine," said Mr. Johnson. "Everything's running like clockwork."

"Not having any troubles with the colonel?"

"Och, no, I just get on with the work, Hamish, and ignore his tantrums. I'm thinking of working here permanently."

"And what has Priscilla to say to that?"

"Actually, it was her idea. She phoned up at

Christmas, worried about what was happening, and when I told her everything, despite her father's frequent interference, was running all right, she suggested I stay on. Suits me. The pay's a damn sight better than at the Lochdubh. When are you coming back?"

"Shortly," said Hamish. "I'd better phone Priscilla. Still at Rogart?"

"Aye, still there and having a grand time, by the sound of it."

Hamish then rang his mother and apologized for not having called sooner, and after asking about various members of the family, asked to speak to Priscilla. "I'm afraid you can't," came his mother's voice. "She's gone off tae the pub with your dad and his friends for a drink."

Hamish briefly tried to imagine the elegant Priscilla propping up some Highland bar with his father and friends and found he could not.

"Where are you, son?" asked his mother.

"In Glasgow."

"At Jean's?"

Jean was Hamish's cousin. "No," said Hamish, "I'm at the Fleur De Lys Hotel in the Great Western Road."

"What are ye doing there? It's awf'y expensive."

"Och, it's chust a wee place," said Hamish, taking

in the luxury of his bedroom surroundings for the first time and feeling like a kept man.

"No, no, I read an article aboot it," came his mother's voice. "How can you afford a place like that?"

Hamish found himself blushing. "It's a long story, Ma. I'll tell ye all about it when I get home."

He talked some more and then rang off. He undressed, got into bed and lay awake for a long time, thinking about the case; and the more he thought about it, the more he decided it must have been an accident and that the weird atmosphere of Eileencraig had put ideas of murder into his head.

But in the morning, over breakfast, he found Harriet was anxious to start the investigations. "I think we should call on Diarmuid," she said. "Where does he live?"

"Morris Place, as I recall."

She took out a street map and studied it. "Why, that's just around the corner. We can walk there."

Morris Place turned out to be a small square of Victorian houses, mostly divided into flats, but Diarmuid, it transpired, owned a whole house. They rang the bell and waited.

After some time, Diarmuid opened the door. He was impeccably dressed in a pin-striped suit, white shirt, and striped silk tie.

"Going out?" asked Hamish.

"I was thinking about going down to the office," said Diarmuid, blocking the doorway, "although I'm pretty tired. I got back from the north in the small hours of the morning. What are you doing here?"

"We just wanted to ask you about Heather."

He heaved an impatient sigh and reluctantly stood back, allowing them to enter. He then led the way to a sitting-room on the first floor. It was thickly carpeted and had a green silk-covered three-piece suite, both armchairs and sofa being ornamented with silk tassels. Heavy green silk fringed curtains were drawn back to let in the pale, grey daylight. A gas fire of simulated logs was flaring away on the hearth. In one corner of the room there was a bar. A low coffee-table stood in front of the fire, its polished oak surface protected with coasters depicting paintings by Impressionist artists. Diarmuid ushered them into chairs and then sat down, adjusting his handsome features into what he obviously considered an expression of suitable grief.

Hamish's first question appeared to surprise him. Was Heather writing a book? Diarmuid said no, although he added that she was always scribbling away at things. "If she had written a book," said Diarmuid, "then she would have got Jessie to type it. Jessie typed all her letters."

Hamish looked at him curiously. "Jessie was *your* secretary. Didn't she resent having to work for your wife as well?"

"Oh, no, she's a good girl, and besides, Heather paid her separately."

"Where is she now?"

"At home."

Hamish took out a small notebook in which he had written all the phone numbers and addresses of his suspects. "Would you mind if I used your phone and gave Jessie a call?"

"Help yourself," said Diarmuid, jerking his head to a white-and-gilt model of an early telephone which stood on a side-table by the window.

Hamish rang Jessie. When she answered, he asked her if Heather had ever asked her to type any pages of manuscript.

"No," said Jessie harshly. "Anything else? I'm busy with the funeral arrangements."

Hamish said no, nothing for the moment, and thoughtfully replaced the receiver.

There seemed to be nothing else to ask Diarmuid. Diarmuid appeared to have forgotten all about going to the office as he ushered them out.

"I feel like giving up," said Harriet gloomily as they left Morris Place. "It's such a long shot, Hamish."

"I'd like to try that editor in New York again," said Hamish. "I've got an idea."

"Well, we can't phone until at least three in the afternoon, when it'll be ten in the morning in New York," pointed out Harriet. "I've got some shopping to do. I'll meet you back at the hotel this afternoon."

Hamish wandered about the city and then ate a solitary lunch, although his mind was not on what he was eating. Bits and pieces of scenes floated through his mind. Jane flushed and angry. John Wetherby electing to stay with Jane. The Carpenters, fat and miserable, trailing off to the station in Oban. Jessie, cool and competent, going off to hire a car in Oban. Diarmuid, relying on his secretary to do everything.

When Harriet came to his hotel room at three in the afternoon, Hamish began to speak immediately, as if he had been discussing the case with her all through lunch. "Look, what about this? Heather actually succeeds in writing a block-buster. Jessie types it and sends it off...but she puts her *own* name on it."

Harriet looked doubtful. "Would such as Jessie recognise a block-buster? Then we're back to means and opportunity. Jessie was not on the island when Heather was killed."

"But Diarmuid was," said Hamish. "That brief fling with Jane could have been a blind."

"He'd need to have been awfully fast to follow Heather all the way over to the other side of the island, run all the way back, and then hop into bed with Jane," pointed out Harriet. "Then striking her down in the dark when he was supposed to be searching for her—well, that's hardly premeditated, and if there's money for a book involved, her death would have to be worked out carefully beforehand."

"There's something there," muttered Hamish. "I can *feel* it."

He picked up the phone and dialled the editor in New York. "I'm sorry to keep bothering you, but it's terribly important that I find out who wrote that book I was asking you about."

"Look, all right, all right," said the editor, "I'll give you the author's name. It's Fiona Stuart."

"Her address?"

The editor's voice was terse. "Sorry, can't do that."

Hamish sadly replaced the receiver. "It's no go. The book was written by someone called Fiona Stuart. Of course it could be a pseudonym."

"Give up, Hamish," said Harriet. "I'm beginning to think it *was* an accident."

"Just one more try," begged Hamish. "Let me speak to that agent of yours."

Harriet sighed but phoned her agent in New York and told the surprised man that a Highland constable called Hamish Macbeth wished to speak to him about that block-buster.

"Well, you're in luck," said the agent as soon as Hamish was on the phone. "The advance publicity is out. It's a saga of vice and crime and passion in the Highlands of Scotland, purple prose, I gather, at its worst. It's a story about a sensitive heroine who is raped by some Highland lord in Chapter One, gang-raped by yuppies in Chapter Two, mugged in Chapter Three. Falls in love with the villain in Chapter Four, and eventually, after bags of sex and mayhem, meets her true love in time for a steamy clinch in the last chapter, her true love being the one who raped her in Chapter One. It's called *Rising Passion* and is reputed to out–Jackie Collins. Fiona Stuart is the name of the author."

Hamish put down the phone and told Harriet what her agent had said. "Hardly a romance," he commented.

"That's romance these days," said Harriet drily. "I bet it all bears no relation to the Highlands whatsoever, and what woman in her right mind would fall in love with a man who'd raped her?"

Hamish put his head in his hands. "There must be some connection." He phoned the editor again. "I told you and told you," snapped the editor, "I can't tell you anything about her. Why don't you phone her agent, for Chrissakes?"

"Can you give me the name of her agent?" asked Hamish. He waited. He was not hopeful at all. He expected the editor to read him out the name of a New York agent. Her American voice twanged over the line. "Here it is. Jessie Maclean, 1256b Hillhead Road, Glasgow."

"Thank you," said Hamish faintly. He put down the phone and turned to Harriet. "Jessie's the agent. How does that work?"

"Easy!" cried Harriet, looking excited. "All my money goes to my agent. He takes his percentage and then sends the rest to me. If he decided to cash the money and disappear abroad, there's nothing I could do about it. Jessie takes Heather's book and acts as agent. She tells Heather she's sent it off to a New York publisher. Maybe, if she was shrewd enough, she'd send several copies round the New York publishers and then play one off against the other. Then she gets the stupendous offer of half a million. She doesn't tell Heather, but she knows the minute the book is published, Heather would know about it."

"But Heather might never have known about it," said Hamish. "She—Jessie, I mean—could just sit back and not offer it to any publisher in Britain. That way there would be a good chance that Heather would never find out about it being published in America."

"But don't you see, Hamish, for half a million she probably sold the world rights."

"Aye, but wait a minute, for that sort of money, wouldn't any editor want to talk to the author?"

"Doesn't need to. All the agent has to say is that the author is very retiring, so retiring she's written under a pseudonym. Jessie can cope with the copy-edited manuscript and the galleys and all that."

"So we've done it," said Hamish, clutching his red hair. "But how do we prove it? There's no Fiona Stuart. It must be Heather's book and Jessie pinched it. But proof? All Jessie has to say is that she wrote the book herself under an assumed name and acted as her own agent. There's no law against that. And even if we could prove it was Heather's book, how could we tie Jessie in with the murder? She wasn't on the island. She didn't know about Heather's death until Diarmuid phoned her."

"Wait a bit," said Harriet. "I've just had an idea. Listen to this. Diarmuid's the sort of weak man who has always had his life run for him by two women,

Heather at home and Jessie in the office. Such a man likes to pretend he's the one who makes all the decisions. What if Jessie *phoned him?*"

Hamish looked at her silently for a long moment and then phoned The Happy Wanderer. It was a bad line and Jane's voice sounded tinny and very far away. Hamish clutched the phone hard as he asked, "Did Diarmuid receive any phone calls on the night Heather's death was discovered?"

"He received one from some woman," came Jane's voice. "He took it in my office."

"So far so good," said Harriet when Hamish told her. "But she wasn't on the island."

They argued on about the pros and cons of the case until Harriet suggested they should see a movie and take their minds off it and return to the problem afresh. But nothing new occurred to either of them. Again, outside her door that night, Hamish wondered whether to try to kiss her, but again she had closed the door on him before he could summon up the courage.

Hamish lay in his bed, tossing and turning, thinking about Eileencraig. He fell into an uneasy sleep about two in the morning, and in his dreams he was being forced off the jetty by Geordie's truck while the maid from The Highland Comfort stood and laughed. He awoke abruptly and switched on the bedside light. That maid, glimpsed briefly, in the shadowy darkness of the stair. Fat with red hair. Wait a bit. What of a Jessie minus horn-rimmed glasses, with pads in her cheeks to fatten them and a red wig on her head? He could hardly wait for breakfast to expound this latest theory to his Watson.

"Won't work," said Harriet. "The hotel would ask for her employment card."

"Not necessarily," said Hamish. "Goodness, if all the employees in hotels in Britain had to have employment cards, well, there'd be self-service. And The Highland Comfort must find it nearly impossible to get staff."

"I can't buy that," retorted Harriet. "There's little enough work on these islands as it is. Look at all the women eager to work for Jane."

"That's different. I bet Jane pays high wages. It's no use phoning up the owner of The Highland Comfort because he's not going to admit to a copper that he hires staff without employment cards. The owner's also the barman and he was complaining about having to do everything himself. Come on, Harriet, we're going to search Jessie's desk."

Diarmuid was at home. He looked surprised at being asked for his office keys but surrendered them without too much of a fuss, which Hamish thought was highly suspicious, because surely a man would expostulate over a continuing investigation by a Highland bobby when his superiors had said the case was closed.

The estate office was in St. Vincent Street in the centre of Glasgow. Already it had a depressed air of failure about it. Outside, above the street, Christmas decorations winked on and off, intensifying the shadowy gloom of the deserted office.

Harriet switched on the lights and looked about. "Well, this is easy. Her desk has her name on it. It's probably locked."

But the desk drawers slid open easily. Typing paper and carbons in the top drawer, headed stationery in the second, files in the third containing correspondence to do with the sale of houses.

"Nothing," said Hamish, disgusted. "Absolutely nothing. We'd better take the keys back to Diarmuid."

A grey drizzle was falling. Christmas was past and people were getting ready for the New Year's Eve celebrations still to come, but the city wore a tired, tawdry air, as if the Calvinistic ghosts of Glasgow were frowning at all this leisure time. The shops were full of people changing gifts and people clutching bits of toys which they had been supposed to assemble at home, but whose instructions they could not follow, probably because the instructions had been badly translated from Hong Kong Chinese. Christmas had done its usual merry work of setting husband against wife, relative against relative, and spreading bad will among men in general. People looked overfed and hung over and desperately worried about how much they had already spent.

A drunk man on the corner was singing, "Have Yourself a Merry Little Christmas." It sounded like a sneer.

"I hate this time of the year," said Hamish. "Hardly any daylight. I wish they'd make Christmas a religious festival and stop all this nonsense of decorations, cards, and gifts. A waste of money." Then he blushed, because he was staying in Glasgow at Harriet's expense and did not want her to think him mean.

"The trouble with Christmas," said Harriet, "is that everyone somehow wants to recapture the glitter and magic of childhood, and it never happens if you look for it. I sometimes think that the people who spend Christmas serving meals to the homeless get the best out of it. Easter's a different matter, but Christmas will always be a pagan festival. The Americans have the best festival—Thanksgiving. No stupid presents, just a good dinner and thanks to God, that's the way Christmas should be."

And having thoroughly depressed each other, Hamish and Harriet made their way back to Diarmuid's to return the keys.

DIARMUID SEEMED ALMOST glad to see them this time. He insisted they come indoors and join him for a drink. Harriet privately thought that the sheer relief of never having to see his wife again had hit him at last. As they sat and talked, Hamish discovered to his amazement that Diarmuid thought his investigations merely a matter of police form. "I never knew you chaps were so thorough," said Diarmuid, sipping a large whisky. "And all because of an accident."

"Well, just to be even more thorough," said Hamish, looking about, "could I inspect Heather's things?"

"I gave her clothes to Oxfam," said Diarmuid. "Is that what you mean?"

He was wearing an open-necked shirt with a silk cravat. He felt the cravat and a worried frown marred his good looks. He stood in front of the mirror over the fireplace and carefully straightened his cravat. He looked at his reflection in the glass and slowly smiled. Hamish thought that Diarmuid had forgotten their very existence. He was looking at what he loved most in the world.

"Not clothes," said Hamish. "I was thinking more of paper and notebooks."

"Mmm?" Diarmuid turned as reluctantly away from his reflection as a lover does from the face of his beloved. "Oh, Jessie was round yesterday afternoon and cleaned the place up. She's got a kind heart. I couldn't bear to do it myself."

"And where did she put the stuff?"

"Into a couple of big garbage bags. Why?"

"Where are the garbage bags?" said Hamish, getting to his feet.

"Downstairs, ready for collection. As a matter of fact, the garbage truck should be along about now. What...?"

He looked in amazement as Hamish and Harriet ran from the room. Then he turned back to the glass and practised a slow, enigmatic smile. He thought that if he could raise one eyebrow like Roger Moore, it would enhance the effect.

Hamish, with Harriet behind him, hurtled out into the street. A small man was just heaving up two bags of garbage to put into the crusher.

"I want these back," shouted Hamish.

The man hurled them down on the pavement, shrugged and followed the now slowly moving garbage truck along the street.

"Treasure trove," said Hamish. "Let's get these back inside and hae a look."

Diarmuid was still practising how to raise that

eyebrow as they entered the sitting-room, Hamish holding the two bags.

"We'll chust go through these," said Hamish.

"Mmm." Diarmuid did not even turn round. There must be some way he could achieve it, but try as he would, both eyebrows kept going up at the same time.

Hamish opened one bag and Harriet the other and they began to sift through the papers. Then Hamish whistled through his teeth. "Look at this."

Harriet took the proffered page.

There was no doubt, it was part of a steamy novel. He took it from her and asked Diarmuid, "Is this your wife's handwriting?"

Diarmuid turned reluctantly away from the mirror. "Yes, that's Heather's, all right. What's this all about?"

"Did you really call Jessie to get her to come to Eileencraig?" asked Hamish. "Or did she phone you?"

Diarmuid looked uneasy. "Well, it's hard to remember. I was in shock."

"It's verra important!"

"Well," mumbled Diarmuid, "she did phone me, as a matter of fact, just to find out how I was getting along, and I told her about Heather's death and she said she would come up right away. She asked me to phone and arrange for a boat to collect her at Oban."

Without asking his permission, Hamish picked up the phone and dialled Jessie's number. There was no reply. "Come on," he said to Harriet. "I've an awful feeling she's gone."

They took a taxi the short distance to Jessie's. It turned out to be a basement flat. He did not even bother to ring the bell. There was a forlorn, deserted air about the place. A woman was leaning against the railings outside talking to another woman. Hamish approached them.

"Have you seen Miss Jessie Maclean this morning?" he asked.

"Aye," said one of the women placidly.

"Do you know where she was going?" Hamish demanded. "Shopping?"

"No' unless it was shop*liftin*'," said the woman, and her friend laughed heartily at her wit. "She hud two suitcases. Yes, she left aboot an hour ago wi' her man."

"What man?"

"Her fella. An accountant, I think that's what she said."

Hamish thought hard. Spain! That was where she had said she might go. He turned to the woman again. "May I use your phone? I am a policeman."

"He must be in trouble again, Betty," said the woman's friend.

"In trouble? What's this about trouble?" asked Hamish feverishly.

"Her man, her boyfriend. He'd done a stretch in prison, I know that," said the woman called Betty, "because Mrs. Queen doon the road's son used tae go tae school wi' him and recognised him and knew all aboot him."

"Phone, please," begged Hamish.

"I'll take him in," said Betty to her friend. She led Hamish up to the front door above Jessie's basement, opened it with her key and let him into a dark hall. Hamish and Harriet waited in an agony of impatience while she fumbled with the key to the door of her ground-floor flat.

"In the hall on the table," said Betty.

The hall was actually a dim corridor. Hamish searched through the phone book and then dialled Glasgow Airport. "Yes," came the metallic voice from the other end in reply to Hamish's question. "There's a plane due to take off for Spain. It's a charter flight delayed for mechanical reasons, but expected to leave any minute now."

Hamish asked to be put through to airport security and introduced himself. "Find out if there's a Jessie Maclean on the flight to Spain, that charter flight."

There was a long wait and then he was told there

was no one of that name on the flight. He turned to the woman who was standing in the hall with a small pocket calculator, obviously working out how much to charge him for the call. "What's the boy-friend's name?" he demanded.

"Macdonald," she said. "Willie Macdonald."

Hamish spoke quickly into the phone and then waited impatiently.

Back came the reply after five agonizing minutes. "Yes, there is a Mr. and Mrs. Macdonald on board."

"There's a murder suspect on that plane," said Hamish. "Get Mr. and Mrs. Macdonald off it and keep them at the airport." Harriet, listening, heard the voice at the other end quack indignantly.

"Yes, yes," said Hamish. "I'll get the proper authority. Don't let them get away!"

He put down the phone and said to Harriet. "Let's go."

"Whit about paying for the call?" demanded Betty. He handed her a pound note and, dragging Harriet after him, ran out and down the street, look-ing for a cab. It was Hogmanay, New Year's Eve, he thought. There would be very few, if any, free cabs about. And then he saw a taxi with its light on rounding a corner and raced for it, with Harriet tumbling after him. He told the cabby to take them to police headquarters.

"How are you going to manage it, Hamish?" asked Harriet anxiously. "You've no proof. I mean, you've proof that she pinched Heather's book but no proof she murdered her."

"I'll get proof," said Hamish, leaning forward and willing the cab to go faster.

At Glasgow police headquarters there were more delays while a detective sergeant phoned Strathbane to establish Hamish's credentials. But Hamish was lucky, Blair was still on holiday, and it was Jimmy Anderson, slightly drunk, who said that Hamish Macbeth was Scotland's answer to Kojak, and if he said there was a murderer at Glasgow Airport, then there surely was.

Soon Harriet found herself crammed into a police car along with Hamish, two detectives, and a policewoman while a carload of four policemen followed behind. They had only gone a little way when Hamish shouted, "Stop!"

The detectives stolidly watched Hamish Macbeth hurtle into a hairdressing salon called Binty's Beauty Parlour. "Whit's he daein'?" asked one laconically. "How should I know?" retorted the other. "Them Highlanders are all daft. Ye cannae figure oot the way their minds work. Maybe it's the mountains. Something tae do wi' the altitude. It affects their brains. Maybe he wants tae look nice for the arrest and is getting his hair cut."

Hamish emerged carrying a paper bag and climbed back into the police car. The detective, driving, said with heavy sarcasm, "Any mair shopping you would like to do?"

"No," said Hamish. "Chust make it quick."

The detective put on the siren and off they went again. Harriet clutched Hamish's hand hard as houses streamed past under the winking lights of the Christmas decorations. At one point, they had to swerve wildly to avoid a drunk weaving across the road. Glasgow had obviously started the New Year's celebrations early.

Hamish gave the detectives an outline of his investigations and Harriet could practically feel disbelief emanating from the square shoulders of the detectives in the front seat, detectives who were used to drunken murders, savage gang fights on the housing estates, but not to sophisticated rigmaroles about books.

Fortunately, it was only a short trip to Glasgow Airport. Harriet blinked in the lights as the detectives, who obviously knew where they were going, led them along a corridor away from the staring passengers and into a room marked "Security."

And there was Jessie Maclean with a tall, weedy man sitting beside her. On a long table in front of them were their suitcases.

Jessie turned white at the sight of Hamish, but she said nothing. "Open the suitcases," ordered Hamish. Jessie slowly produced the keys. Hamish searched one of Jessie's pale-blue suitcases carefully after examining the passports. Their passports, which showed they were married, had been issued only a few weeks before.

Then he found the contract for the book and sheets of headed paper, "Jessie Maclean, Literary Agent." He silently took Jessie's handbag from her and tipped out the contents. In it was a banker's draft for the money.

Jessie glared up at him after stuffing everything back into her bag and clutching it tight. "That money's mine," she said. "I earned it. I wrote the book."

Hamish put both hands on the other side of the table and leaned forward.

"What were you doing on Eileencraig the day Heather Todd was murdered?"

"You're daft!" screamed Jessie. "You all saw me arrive. You can't keep me. Let me out of here..."

Hamish smiled and slowly straightened up. He turned round and took the bag he had brought out of the hairdressers' from Harriet. He turned back and opened it and edged out of the bag a handful of red hair, a wig.

Harriet reflected dizzily that she had read of

people turning green but had never seen it before that moment. Jessie's face was an awful colour under the harsh glare of the strip lighting overhead.

She rounded on her husband. "You stupid bastard!" she screamed. "You told me you'd burnt it." She tried to rake his face with her nails and was dragged off, still screaming, by the detectives to a corner of the room, where she suddenly subsided into noisy sobs.

"Well, Willie Macdonald?" demanded Hamish. "You'd better tell all or you'll find yourself on a murder charge as well."

"Don't tell him," gulped Jessie between sobs.

"It wisnae anything to do wi' me," said Willie, looking down at the table. "Jessie told me the auld bag had written a book but didnae want anyone to know about it in case it got rejected, so she asked Jessie tae type it oot and put her name down as literary agent. Jessie thought it was a right load o' rubbish. Then she got a phone call frae New York offering her a half a million on behalf of her client. She thought the whole thing up hersel'. Naethin' tae dae wi' me. She telt me she killed her. She hid ootside that health farm and watched fur the opportunity."

His thin, weak face suddenly looked up at Hamish in puzzlement. "But how did ye find the wig? I burnt it, like she said, in a bin in the garden at the back o' her flat."

"And so you probably did," said Hamish pleasantly. "This is a wig I bought at a hairdressers' on the road here."

"You bastard," whispered Jessie suddenly. "I could have got away with it."

One of the detectives read the charges. "We'll take them back to headquarters and get their statements. We'd better get your statement as well, Macbeth." He held out his hand. "Detective Sergeant Peter Sinclair, Macbeth. It's been a pleasure watching ye work. But man, man, ye took a chance buying that wig."

Hamish shook hands with him, and then, putting an arm around Harriet's shoulders, he followed police and prisoners outside to the car.

WHEN THEY FINALLY emerged from police headquarters, all the city bells were ringing. A drunk reeled past, red-eyed under the street lights. "Happy New Year," he shouted.

"And so it is," said Hamish. He put his arms around Harriet and held her close and bent his head to kiss her. He finally raised his head and looked down at her curiously. She was stiff in his arms and she had only endured that kiss.

"I think," said Harriet breathlessly, "that we should call on Diarmuid."

"Why?" demanded Hamish, made cross by rejection. "The police'll have phoned him."

"Well, it's New Year's Eve and I have a feeling he'll be all alone. Did you notice the times we were there that the phone did not ring once? No one calling to offer their condolences?"

"Very well, then," said Hamish sulkily. "But I can tell you this, Harriet. I wish he *had* done it."

They couldn't get a cab, so Hamish went back into the police station and begged a lift in a squad car.

As he rang Diarmuid's doorbell and waited, hoping that the man wouldn't answer, he wondered why Harriet had disliked that kiss. She was attracted to him, he was sure of that. He was just about to turn away, relieved, when the hall light went on and then Diarmuid answered the door. He was wearing pale-blue silk pyjamas and a white satin dressing-gown with his initials monogrammed in gold on one pocket.

"Hamish and Harriet," he exclaimed. "How good of you to come. This is a terrible business. A terrible business. The police told me about it."

"Have you no one with you?" asked Harriet as they followed him up the stairs and into the sitting-room. Diarmuid lit the gas fire. "No," he said. "It's with it being New Year's Eve. I phoned a few people but they were all busy. Can you tell me about it, Hamish? All I got from the police was that Jessie had murdered my wife and that they would be calling on me in the morning to take a statement."

Hamish sat down. He looked curiously at Harriet, a question in his eyes. She flushed slightly and looked away.

"It's like this," said Hamish in a flat voice. "Your wife wrote a steamy romance..."

"Heather? She never would!"

"I don't think she thought of it as popular writing," said Harriet. "She probably set out to write a literary novel and that's the way it came out. She must have read an awful lot of that kind of book, and with enjoyment, too. You can't really write what you don't like to read."

Diarmuid put a finger to his brow and frowned. Does the man never stop acting? thought Hamish angrily.

"She did read a lot of them," he volunteered, "but it was because she said she was writing a speech to give to the Workers' Party on decadence and the decline of moral standards in popular fiction."

What had Heather really been like under all that political pose? wondered Harriet. She must have needed a fantasy life to read and enjoy and absorb so many sexy romances.

"Anyway," said Hamish, anxious to get this visit over with quickly, "the police telephoned the owner of The Highland Comfort this evening. Jessie, padded out and wearing a red wig, just walked in about two weeks before the murder. She said she wanted a working holiday and he was glad to get her. No, he didn't ask for her employment card. He told the police that Jessie had told him her employment card was being sent on. He said Jane had spoiled things for him by paying high wages. He paid abysmal wages, as it turned out, so the island women who used to work for him preferred to wait until the season started and work for Jane."

"What name did Jessie use when she was working there?" asked Harriet.

"That's where I could kick myself," said Hamish ruefully. "She went under the name of Fiona Stuart, Heather's pseudonym.

"She said she didn't mean to murder Heather. She had some idea that if she told Heather, they could split the proceeds fifty-fifty, and she meant to suggest to her that they didn't let Diarmuid know. On her afternoon off, she hid behind that pillbox and saw us all coming out. Then she saw Heather and you, Diarmuid, having that row and Heather stalking off on her own. She followed her and when she considered they were both far enough away from the health farm, she caught up with her. Heather was amazed to see the efficient secretary, rising, it seemed, out of the moorland, wearing a red wig and with her cheeks and figure padded out.

"They walked together towards the west coast and that crag, and as they went, Jessie told Heather about her plan to split the proceeds. Heather was very excited, elated. She said her book was a literary work of art. She babbled on about possible lecture tours in the States. Jessie interrupted at last by asking her if they had a deal. Heather looked at her in surprise and said of course they hadn't a deal.

"Jessie then asked bitterly if she could at least depend on her agent's fee of fifteen per cent. Heather sneered that Jessie was nothing but a little secretary and was paid well for her duties and there was no need for her to get greedy. By this time she was standing on that crag. She looked out to sea and began to talk again about how famous she would be.

"Jessie said she suddenly thought of all the drudgery, all the work she had done for Heather, and she saw red. She saw a large, sharp rock lying on the ground at her feet. She picked it up and smashed it into the side of Heather's neck. Heather fell down on that little beach and lay still. Jessie threw the rock into the sea and ran all the way back to the hotel and waited until she heard the news next day that Heather's body had been found. She phoned you, Diarmuid, saying she was in Glasgow and you told her about Heather and she offered to come up. She was working in the bar that night and that was where you phoned to Angus Macleod to ask him to go and pick up Jessie. Jessie then approached Angus and said she was fed up with the hotel and wanted to leave, and as he was going to Oban anyway, he could take her.

"Once in Oban, she went to lodgings she had already hired and packed up the wig and the padding. Now the thing is, I do not think the murder was unpremeditated, because she had all the business papers and copies of Heather's will and insurance in a case already with her. All she had to do was travel back with Angus and then act the part of perfect secretary."

"Did her husband put her up to it?" asked Harriet.

"Husband? What husband?" demanded Diarmuid.

"She had married a criminal, Willie Macdonald," said Hamish. "He had just got out of prison after serving a sentence for defrauding the company he had worked for as an accountant. He would know about cashing bank drafts and everything like that. But no, Jessie was the sole planner of the whole thing."

"Goodness," said Diarmuid weakly, "and to think I have had a murderess working for me!"

Suddenly he leaned forward and said eagerly, "Heather left me everything in her will. Of course, up till now 'everything' was nothing but debts. Will I get the money for the book?"

Hamish looked at him with distaste. "Oh, yes," he said.

"And although all this publicity will be very painful," put in Harriet, "it should help sales immensely."

Diarmuid rubbed his hands. "Just wait till I tell my friends."

"Yes, now you've money, you'll probably see them all again," said Hamish cynically, but Diarmuid wasn't listening.

He crossed to the bar. "Well," he said cheerfully, "this does call for a celebration."

Hamish felt he had had enough. "No, we must go. Coming, Harriet?"

Harriet stood up reluctantly. Hamish was going to ask her questions she didn't want to answer.

They walked silently together to their hotel. This time, Hamish followed Harriet into her room and looked down at her seriously. "I am not in the way of making passes when I think they will not be welcome," said Hamish. "So what happened?"

"Sit down, Hamish," said Harriet. Hamish sat on the edge of the bed and she sat beside him and took one of his hands in hers.

"I'm to blame." Harriet looked up at him and there was the glitter of tears in her large grey eyes. "I was ... I am attracted to you. I should have let you know before, but it was all so exciting, the murder investigation, I mean."

"Let me know what?"

"I am engaged to be married. My future husband, Neil, is an officer in the British Army. He's due back from Hong Kong."

Hamish removed his hand. "When?"

"In London, tomorrow. I'm travelling down on the morning plane."

"You might have let me know," said Hamish stiffly.

"Oh, Hamish..."

He rose. "I, too, will leave in the morning," he said without looking at her. "Thank you for all your generosity and help."

"Hamish..."

But he walked out and closed the door behind him.

He went to his room and set the alarm in case he slept in. He would catch the train to Edinburgh in the morning and from there take the train to Inverness. He lay down on the bed, fully dressed, and tried not to feel like a fool.

And then the phone beside his ear rang sharp and insistent. He reached out and picked it up.

"Hamish!" came Priscilla Halburton-Smythe's voice.

"Priscilla." He sat up.

"I've been phoning and phoning," cried Priscilla. "Where have you been?"

"Out. It's a long story. What's wrong?"

"I just wanted to wish you a happy New Year."

"Oh, aye, Happy New Year, Priscilla. Still with my folks?"

"No, back at the hotel. Towser's here. He's fine but missing you. I had the best Christmas ever. When do you get back?"

"I'm catching the Inverness train from Edinburgh tomorrow. I'll be in Inverness just after eight. I'll probably stay the night with my friends, Iain and Biddy, out at Torgormack, and then catch the sprinter in the morning."

There was a silence and then Priscilla said, "I'll come and fetch you if you like. Tomorrow. At Inverness station."

"That would be grand, Priscilla."

There was another silence.

Then Priscilla's voice, sharp and anxious. "What's up, Hamish?"

"It wass the end of a murder inquiry," said Hamish. "I feel flat. I'll tell you all about it when I see you."

"How come you are staying at such an expensive hotel? Glasgow police being generous?"

"No, I'll tell you about that as well. I'd better get some sleep."

"All right, Hamish. Goodbye."

Priscilla slowly replaced the receiver. Something had happened to Hamish Macbeth and she was sure it was nothing to do with the murder case he had been on.

Chapter Eight

*Good breeding consists in concealing how much
we think of ourselves and how little we think of
the other person.*

—Mark Twain

The tinny alarm bell shrilled in Hamish's ear and he
started up. He had fallen asleep still dressed, and he
felt hot and dirty. He had a shower and changed and
then went along to Harriet's room and tapped on the
door.

He felt he had behaved very badly. She had not
thrown herself at him. He had read too much into
simple friendliness and he had no right to be angry
with her.

There was no reply to his knock and all at once
he knew she had left. He looked at his watch. Seven
in the morning.

He went down to the reception desk. The night

porter, still on duty, answered his query by saying that, yes, she had left. There was a letter for him. Hamish glanced at it. He could not bear to read it and shoved it into his pocket.

He had breakfast and then packed and made his way to the station to catch the Edinburgh train, stopping off on the way to buy a bottle of perfume for Priscilla. He felt he should have gone to visit his relatives and stayed with them in Glasgow for another night, but could not bring himself to do so. Before boarding the train, he bought the morning papers. The news of the arrest of Jessie and her husband had occurred too late for the first editions. He wondered if he would be mentioned in the later editions and then decided, probably not. Glasgow police would take the credit, not out of vanity, but simply to avoid long-winded explanations to the press about how some holidaying Highland copper came to solve the mystery.

He had had very little sleep and nodded off, only waking when a shout of "Waverly, next stop!" heralded his arrival in Edinburgh.

A group raising money for famine relief were singing Christmas carols in a corner of the station. It seemed almost indecent to hear Christmas carols in the new year.

Hamish lugged his travelling-bag to the Inverness

train. Every seat was taken and he had to stand as far as Stirling. When he was finally seated, he remembered Harriet's letter and reluctantly pulled it out. "Dear Hamish," he read. "Do not think too badly of me. I should have told you at the beginning that I was engaged. It was all my fault. I am sorry our great adventure had to end this way and please don't feel too badly rejected. Think of me sometimes. I shall certainly never forget you. Love, Harriet."

He shrugged and put the letter back in his pocket. As the towns slid past on the road to the north, Perth, Blair Atholl, Dalwhinnie, Kingussie, Aviemore, he felt the whole business receding. Eileencraig with Jane and her health farm, Geordie and his truck, seemed a million miles away. He wondered briefly if Jane and John Wetherby would remarry.

And then he arrived in Inverness. Snow was falling as he walked along the platform, the sea-gulls of Inverness were screaming overhead, and there was Priscilla, standing at the end of the platform with Towser on a leash.

She dropped the leash and Towser came bounding up to meet him, ridiculous tail wagging energetically, scrabbling at Hamish in delight with large muddy paws.

"He looks well," said Hamish, dropping a kiss

on Priscilla's cold cheek, "and so do you." She was almost restored to her former beauty. Her golden hair had a healthy shine and the hollows had left her cheeks.

"Your mother's cooking," said Priscilla. "I was going to take you out to dinner in Inverness, and then I thought you would probably like to go straight home."

"Aye, that would be grand," said Hamish, his face lighting up in a smile.

"So," said Priscilla as she drove the hotel Range Rover out over the bridge and took the road to the north, "tell me about the case."

Hamish began, reluctantly at first, and then all at once he was back on Eileencraig. He described all the guests vividly, with the exception of Harriet Shaw.

"And so you went to Glasgow," said Priscilla, "and stayed at that expensive little hotel. Unlike you, Hamish. Hamish?"

"I wasnae paying," mumbled Hamish.

"And who was?"

"Harriet Shaw."

"So you were a kept man," commented Priscilla coolly. "What was she like?"

"Who?"

"Hamish!"

"Well, nice, ordinary, straightforward. Writes cookery books."

"I know, I have several of her books. She's very good. What prompted the generous offer, or should I ask?"

"She wass helping me wi' my inquiries," said Hamish stiffly. "If she hadn't volunteered to pay, I couldn't even have afforded a more modest hotel."

"You could have stayed with Jean," pointed out Priscilla, an edge to her voice.

Hamish cursed under his breath. Of course, after a stay with his family, Priscilla would know the names of all his relatives.

"Look," he said, "it chust happened. She was helping me wi' my inquiries."

"Oh, yes," said Priscilla flatly. "How old is she?"

"About forty-five."

"As old as that? And where is she now?"

"Gone to meet her fiancé in London."

"Oh." There was a long pause. Then Priscilla said cheerfully, "I remember seeing her on television. Pleasant-looking woman. Certainly looks a lot younger than forty-five."

"Not when you meet her," said Hamish, thrusting a knife into his memory of Harriet in order to keep the atmosphere between himself and Priscilla light.

"Well, it's all very odd," remarked Priscilla.

"What is?" demanded Hamish, hoping she would not pursue his relationship with Harriet Shaw any further.

"This Heather Todd, the one who was killed. Imagine writing a whole novel and your husband not even knowing about it."

"He said she was always scribbling at something and he thought she was preparing a speech for the Workers' Party."

"Still, to keep up that Communist front and yet relish reading romances. A sort of double life. Perhaps she is to be pitied."

"You didn't meet her," said Hamish. "She was a nasty, irritating woman. When I told her I was in forestry because I didn't want her to know I was a policeman, she hectored me about the destruction of the environment until I began to want to see the whole world covered in concrete. She had that sort of effect. She was a woman begging to be murdered."

"That's what I meant," said Priscilla. "Surely to be pitied. And Jane? Are all her friends like me, mere acquaintances?"

"So it seems."

"And have you thought about that rock that Jane said nearly killed her?"

"No, why?" Hamish sounded puzzled. "I took a

good look at the bathroom heater and decided the builder had been right. It was an accident, so I never got around to asking her closely about the rock or bothering to see where it had happened."

"Think of it this way," said Priscilla as they drove over the Dornoch Firth bridge, "Heather liked to dress like Jane. Jessie was no doubt prowling the island on her time off long before the day of the murder, waiting for an opportunity to get rid of Heather. There's little daylight this time of year. She could have seen Jane in the darkness, mistaken her for Heather, and shied a rock at her. Now if that had happened, and she had succeeded in killing Jane, it would really have complicated things."

"I should have questioned that further," said Hamish ruefully. "In fact, I've been verra lucky all round. If Harriet Shaw hadn't been there, and herself an author to let me know all about the selling of books, and if Jessie hadn't cracked at the sight of that red wig, it would have been difficult to prove. But the biggest mistake of all was not asking at the hotel what name the maid had used. Can you imagine? Jessie used the name Fiona Stuart, Heather's pseudonym."

"But even if you had found out earlier, it wouldn't have meant a thing," pointed out Priscilla. "It wouldn't have meant anything unless you had got the idea about the book."

"That's true," agreed Hamish. "But what about you, Priscilla? I'm surprised you stayed with my family for so long."

"I had the best Christmas I've ever had, Hamish." Priscilla left the main road and drove the car expertly towards the Struie Pass. "So easygoing. Such fun. And your mother is a darling."

"What about Aunt Hannah?"

"Well, that's the odd thing. She was quite miffed that you weren't there and felt you had deliberately snubbed her."

"That's her way," said Hamish. "She always did like making people feel guilty."

"But she didn't manage to spoil the fun. I slept for hours and hours and ate huge meals, played Scrabble and Monopoly, went for walks with your brothers and sisters, and went to the pub with your father. You are lucky, Hamish. I often wish I had brothers and sisters."

"You'll have children of your own one day," said Hamish. There was a sudden constraint between them and they drove most of the rest of the way back to Lochdubh in silence.

When they were driving along the waterfront at Lochdubh, Priscilla said awkwardly, "You left me the keys, so I took the liberty of preparing a meal for us."

"That was kind of you. Thank you."

Towser frolicked before them into the kitchen and stood wagging his tail next to the cooker and looking up at them hopefully. "I'd better feed the dog first," said Priscilla. "You go through the living room, Hamish, and put your feet up. The fire's made up. All you have to do is put a match to it."

Hamish took off his coat and hung it up. He went into the living-room and lit the fire. Then he remembered he had bought Priscilla a bottle of perfume before boarding the train in Glasgow and was glad he had done so because there was a pile of Christmas presents from his family lying on the table and also one with a card that he recognized from the handwriting as being from Priscilla.

"I've got you a present," he shouted. "It's in my coat pocket."

"Thank you, Hamish." Priscilla went to his coat, which was hanging behind the back door, and felt in the pockets and then pulled out a small square box. As she did so, a crumpled piece of paper fell out and dropped to the floor. She picked it up and automatically smoothed it out. It was Harriet's letter to Hamish. She shouldn't have read it, but she did.

So, thought Priscilla, reading between the lines, Hamish made a pass, and a heavy one, too.

"Like it?" called Hamish.

"What?" Priscilla feverishly tore off the wrapping paper from the present. "Yes. Lovely. My favorite French perfume." She carefully put the crumpled letter back in his pocket. Towser was eating with relish, his tail still wagging, delighted to be home.

With nervous efficient movements, Priscilla grilled a steak, fried potatoes, mushrooms, and tomatoes, put the lot on a tray and carried it through.

"I'm being fair spoiled," said Hamish with a grin. Then he said, "Where's yours?"

"I'm not really hungry," said Priscilla, "and I've just remembered I have a lot to do. I'd better go."

"Oh, can't you stay for a bit? I thought Johnson was handling everything."

"No, no. Must run. 'Bye, Hamish." And she fairly ran from the room and the next minute he heard the kitchen door slam.

He felt very flat. He had not even opened his presents.

Women!

SAVOR THE FLAVORS OF SCOTLAND—
WITH ANOTHER
HAMISH MACBETH MYSTERY
BY **M. C. BEATON!**

*Please turn the page
for a preview of*

Death of a Policeman

A watched pot never boils.

—Mid-nineteenth-century proverb

The fact that all the police forces in Scotland were to be amalgamated into one large force struck terror into police headquarters in Strathbane. It was said that all over Scotland three thousand auxiliary jobs would be lost, which would mean more work for the actual police themselves. Then they would start chopping heads of the very police force itself.

Only one man was happy about the news— Detective Chief Inspector Blair. Surely this might be the opportunity to get rid of Police Sergeant Hamish Macbeth and winkle him out of his cosy station in Lochdubh. He could not understand how Hamish had been able to hang on with local police stations closing down all over Scotland.

But he experienced a setback when he broached

the idea to his chief, Superintendent Daviot. "Sutherland is a huge county," said Daviot, "and it is surely economical to have Macbeth cover all of it."

"But most of the time, he and his sidekick, Fraser, just mooch around doing nothing," complained Blair.

"We have no proof of that," said Daviot severely. "You should be worried about your own job."

"Whit!"

"I am sure we will have officials soon crawling all over us to see what they can cut," said Daviot.

Blair took himself off to the pub to crouch over a double whisky and try to work out a plan. If he could prove that Hamish Macbeth did little, then he could send a report in to the new authorities. But who would be low enough to spy on Macbeth?

After another double whisky, his brain seemed to clear. Cyril Sessions was a fairly new constable, nicknamed Romeo because of his good looks. Shortly after his arrival from Perth, Blair had uncovered evidence that Cyril had been enjoying the favours of a prostitute, without paying her a penny. She had finally cracked and reported Cyril. Blair got the complaint and confronted Cyril. Cyril had pleaded and begged and said he would do anything if Blair made the complaint go away.

Cunningly, Blair decided to keep this ally in the

bank, so to speak, until such time as he would need to draw on him. He phoned headquarters and asked Cyril to join him.

Women in the pub stared appreciatively at Cyril when he entered. He was of medium height with glossy black hair, blue eyes in a square handsome face, and a muscular figure.

"Sit down, my lad," said Blair. "I've a wee job for you. I want evidence that Hamish Macbeth in Lochdubh does bugger all when it comes to policing."

"Isn't that the man who's got a grand reputation for solving murders?"

"It was me that solved them," said Blair, "while that slimy toad took the credit. You owe me a favour, or do I need to remind you that I had to threaten that brass nail to keep her painted mouth shut?"

"Brass nail?"

"Where have you been? Brass nail. Screw. Get it? That prossy you were banging."

"Oh, aye. That."

"Aye, that. Here's what you've got tae do. Take a fishing holiday in Lochdubh and get photos of Macbeth lounging around. His policeman, Dick Fraser, often sleeps in a deck chair in the front garden. Get a good shot o' that. Macbeth doesn't know you, so you can get real close. Chat with the locals. Pick up gossip."

"I don't fish."

"Well, rambling or something like that. The highlands are fu' o' hairy-legged bastards farting ower the hills."

"When do I start?"

"Next week'll do. I want this done and dusted before numpties from the new police arrangement descend on us."

Cyril looked at him shrewdly. "Have you tried this before?"

Blair shifted his fat haunches on the barstool. He had, in fact, and it had ended with his spy nearly getting killed. But he had no intention of telling Cyril anything about it.

"No, just thought o' it," he said. "Get moving and fix that holiday."

HAMISH WAS ACTUALLY working at that moment. Lairg sheep sales are the biggest in Europe and he was policing them with Dick at his side. Because of the size of the sales, Strathbane had sent up two policemen to assist him. The importance of the yearly event meant that crofters were often dressed in the sort of finery people thought were the reserve of tourists: deer stalkers, tall crooks, kilts and sporrans.

Hamish and Dick strolled into the beer tent late

in the day and found their other two colleagues. "Everyone upset about the new Scottish police force?" asked Hamish, joining them.

"You can say that again," said one of them. "Take off the civilian staff, and think o' the extra paperwork."

"And how's my dear friend Blair?" asked Hamish.

The other policeman sniggered, "I think he's in lurv."

"Who's the lucky lady?"

"It's a bloke. Fairly new copper called Cyril Sessions. Real handsome chap. Blair's been seen drinking with him all over the place. Can't get enough of his company."

As THEY WALKED out of the beer tent, Dick said sententiously, "It does happen, you know."

"What does?" asked Hamish.

"Fellows when they get on a bit. They wake up to the fact that they prefer other blokes to their missus."

"Oh, aye? Well, the only love affair Blair's ever had is with the booze. He's plotting something."

"Do you mind if I hurry off?" said Dick anxiously. "I'm due down in Strathbane."

"Another quiz?"

"Aye, and the prize is a brand new Volvo."

"Off you go. Things are quiet here."

HAMISH SWITCHED ON the television that evening. Dick had such a reputation for winning quiz competitions that he was surprised they let him on.

The questions seemed to be very difficult. Six contestants were quickly whittled down to two, Dick and a shabby old man. And then Dick lost at the last question: how long does it take light from the moon to reach the earth?

The old man said quickly, "One-point-twenty-six seconds." There was a roll of drums and cheers from the audience as he was led to the gleaming new car.

Hamish waited up until a weary Dick arrived home. "Not like you to lose," said Hamish. "That must be the first time."

"I couldnae do it to him," said Dick.

"What?"

"He was an auld crofter. He'd never been on one of thae quiz shows before. The stories o' hardship he told me in the green room. It would ha' been wicked not to let the poor auld soul win."

"What was his name again?"

"Henry McQueen. Got a bittie o' a place outside Bonar Bridge."

"I wonder if there's anything on the computer about him," said Hamish.

"Why?"

"Just a hunch. I've got a feeling I saw him at the sheep sales."

Dick followed Hamish into the police office. Hamish switched on the computer and searched for Henry McQueen's name. "There's something here from last year's *Highland Times*," said Hamish, clicking it open. "There you are. I thought I'd heard of him. He took top price for his lambs two years running. You were conned. Oh, here's another link. Five years ago he came out top on *Mastermind*. Subject, the Epistles of St. Paul."

"I'll murder the auld creep," raged Dick.

"Oh, leave it. I'm sure he'll crop up again," said Hamish soothingly, "and then you can wipe the floor with him."

THE FOLLOWING DAY, Cyril checked into Mrs. Mackenzie's bed and breakfast on the waterfront at Lochdubh. He dumped his haversack in a small room and wondered how long he could put up with pretending to be a rambler, particularly as he had arrived in his car. He had pointed out to Blair that he was surely not going to be able to follow Macbeth around on foot.

The room was at the back of the house. It was cold. There was a meter on the wall with a sign saying that pound coins had to be deposited for electricity. The bed was narrow and covered in rough blankets under a pink candlewick spread. A print of Jesus feeding the multitude with loaves and fishes hung over the blocked-up fireplace. Underneath was the legend "His Eye Is on the Sparrow." On a rickety table by the bed was a large Bible. The room was fairly dark. Cyril popped a coin in the meter and switched on the light in a glass bowl above his head full of dead flies. He hung his clothes in the curtained alcove that served as a wardrobe. There was neither a phone nor a television set. The only reason, he thought, that she got any customers was because Mrs. Mackenzie charged cheap rates.

He decided to go out for a walk around the village and start work.

The day outside was warmer than his room. A pale October sun shone down on a row of whitewashed cottages fronting the sea loch. It looked like a picture postcard. Cyril walked towards the harbour. He brightened when he saw a pub. He would start with a drink and see what he could find out from the locals. There was a silence when he entered. He ordered a vodka and tonic.

A small man in tight clothes materialised at his elbow and said, "Are you on holiday?"

"Yes," said Cyril. "I'm Jamie Mackay up from Perth."

"Archie Maclean," said the little man.

"Let me buy you a drink," said Cyril, "and maybe we could sit over at that table by the window. I'd like to get to know a bit about the village."

Archie ordered a double whisky. Cyril realised that Blair had said nothing about paying for his work. Conversation rose again as they made their way to the table.

"So what are you doing here?" asked Archie.

"I came up by car, but I might do a bit of walking."

Archie's sharp blue eyes in his nut-brown face dropped to look at Cyril's highly polished black shoes. "I hope you've got boots with you," he said. "You won't get far in those."

"Yes, I've got boots," said Cyril. He wondered why the little man wore such tight clothes, not knowing that Archie's wife washed all his clothes so that they shrank.

"So, much crime around here?" asked Cyril.

"No, it's fair quiet."

"I saw a police station. Not much for a copper to do up here."

"Hamish Macbeth, the police sergeant, covers a big part o' Sutherland," said Archie. "He's got a lot tae do. Thanks for the drink, laddie. Got tae go."

HAMISH WAS SEATED at the kitchen table when Archie burst through the door. "What's up?" asked Hamish.

"'Member the time when that scunner Blair put a copper on yer tail to report on ye?"

"As if it were yesterday," said Hamish. "Has he sent another?"

"Could be," said Archie, sitting down at the table. "Could I hae wan o' your espresso coffees? The wifie doesnae hold wi' coffee."

"That's Dick's machine. I don't know how to operate it. I'll fetch him. He's sleeping in the garden."

Hamish strolled round to the front of the police station just in time to see the tall figure of Cyril snapping a photograph of Dick asleep in his deck chair. He nipped round onto the road and confronted Cyril. "What's so special about a photograph of a man in a deck chair?" asked Hamish.

"I'm a bit of an amateur photographer," said Cyril. "I thought I'd enter it for a competition and call it 'Sleeping Policeman.'"

"Visiting?"

"Yes. Good place for walks."

"Where are you staying?" asked Hamish.

"Mrs. Mackenzie's. I'll be getting along."

Cyril strode off. Hamish stared after him. Then he went into the office and phoned detective Jimmy Anderson.

"How are things up in peasantville?" asked Jimmy.

"Weird."

"It's aye weird up there."

"There's this fellow turned up and took a photo of Dick asleep in the garden. Handsome chap with curly black hair, tall, blue eyes, little half-moon scar above the right eye, but with policeman's shoes on and black socks. Says he's going to be going for walks. Anyone missing from headquarters that looks like that?"

"There's one smarmy bastard who sucks up to Blair. Cyril Sessions."

"I knew it!" exclaimed Hamish. "Blair is out to get proof that there's no crime up here. I'll get that photo back somehow."

Hamish woke Dick up and explained the situation. He ended by saying, "Let's see if we can lose the cheil for an hour. Give Archie a mug o' espresso first."

They walked over to the harbour fifteen minutes later, where Archie Maclean was sitting on a bollard, rolling a cigarette. "No tourists today?" asked Hamish. Fishing stocks were dwindling, and so Archie supplemented his income by taking tourists on trips round the loch.

"I've only got a couple. They'll be along in a minute."

"Do me a favour. Yon chap you met in the pub is one o' Blair's snoops. He'll be hanging around. He's staying at Mrs. Mackenzie's. Offer him a free trip in your boat."

"Aye, right. Want me to tip him ower the side?"

"No, just keep him away. If he's got his camera with him, try to stage an accident to the camera that makes it look as if it's his fault."

ARCHIE SCURRIED OFF. He found Cyril outside Mrs. Mackenzie's. Cyril was delighted to accept. It would be a chance to find out more about Macbeth.

Hamish stood at his living-room window, watching, until he saw the fishing boat sail out into the loch. Then he hurried along to Mrs. Mackenzie's bed and breakfast.

Before he got there, he met the Currie sisters, twins Nessie and Jessie, on the waterfront. They were very much alike. Although the day was sunny, there was a nip in the air, and so they had reverted to their winter wear of camel-hair coats, headscarves, and brogues.

"Grand day," said Hamish. "Have you seen the newcomer?"

"We have that," said Nessie. "Like a fillum star."

"Fillum star," echoed the Greek chorus that was Jessie.

"It's refreshing to find a young man who kens so much about the Bible," said Hamish. "He's out with Archie, but when he gets back, you should invite him to tea. Right religious, he is."

"We'll do that," said Nessie. "It will be nice to talk to a clean young man instead o' a lazy philanderer like yourself."

"Like yourself," came her sister's echo.

Hamish walked on and knocked at the door of the bed and breakfast. Mrs. Mackenzie was a small woman wearing a flower-patterned overall with her hair tied up in a headscarf. The lines on her face were permanently set in disapproval.

"Whit?" she demanded.

"I would like a look at the newcomer's room," said Hamish. "We've had a tip-off."

"Then he can pack his bags and get out."

"No, no," said Hamish soothingly. "Don't tell him I called. Chust a routine enquiry. You don't want to go losing a paying customer at this time of year. Chust a wee peek in his room."

"Oh, all right. Top o' the stairs on the left. The door isnae locked. I was up there cleaning."

Hamish nipped up the stairs and into Cyril's room. There was a computer lying on the bed, but what he wanted was the camera. There was no sign of it. He could only hope that Archie would find a way to get rid of it.

ARCHIE LET HIS mate, Ally Harris, take the wheel while he pointed out various landmarks to the two tourists, a husband and wife, and Cyril. Cyril was standing at the side of the boat, his camera slung round his neck.

Moving behind him, Archie took out a sharp knife and sliced almost through the strap at the back of Cyril's neck.

He said, "If youse will look ower the side, that's where the kelpie is supposed tae live."

"What's a kelpie?" asked the female.

"It's a creature that appears as a sea horse and sometimes changes into a beautiful wumman," said Archie. "It goes after wee bairns. It gets them to stroke it and it's adhesive and when they stick to it, it drags them down into the loch and eats them. It's supposed to live right down there. Lean right ower and you'll maybe see it."

Cyril and the tourists leaned over. "There is

something down there," said Cyril excitedly. A black shape could be seen moving in the murky depths. His camera was swinging from his neck by the strap. Just as he was reaching for it, the strap broke and his camera dropped down into the water.

A seal surfaced and stared up at them as Cyril let out a wail of dismay.

"You should ha' got yourself wan o' thae wee yins you can carry in your pocket," said Archie. "I hivnae seen wan like that in years. If you go to Patel's shop, you can buy wan o' thae cheap throwaway ones."

"It was a friend's camera," said Cyril. He cursed Blair, who had given him an old Rolleiflex camera out of storage at headquarters, saying it was better than any newfangled one. He did have a Canon pocket one inside his jacket. At least he would be more comfortable using that.

ARCHIE TELEPHONED HAMISH to say that Cyril's camera was now somewhere at the bottom of the loch, and Hamish heaved a sigh of relief.

Before, when he had been under threat, he had manufactured a crime wave with the help of the locals. But Hamish was feeling lazy, enjoying the rare good weather of the autumn.

* * *

CYRIL HAD READ up on Hamish's successful cases and knew that several had taken place in the town of Braikie. The following day, he decided to visit the town, hoping the residents there might have less favourable ideas about Hamish than the villagers had. He had gone to the village stores and after leaning on the counter, talking about the weather, he had asked the owner, Mr. Patel, what he thought of the local policeman. Mr. Patel had smiled and launched on a paean of praise about Hamish.

Cyril had then gone to the Italian restaurant for dinner and quizzed the waiter, Willie Lamont. His heart sank when it turned out that Hamish was godfather to Willie's child. Was no one going to criticise the man?

But in Braikie, his hopes sank lower. The people he talked to did not know Hamish personally but knew his reputation for solving murders and seemed to be proud to have such a policeman looking after them.

He was passing the library when he noticed a sign outside saying there were books for sale. Cyril decided to buy some light reading and walked into the Victorian gloom of the building.

Hetty Dunstable, the librarian, saw a handsome man looking around and teetered forward on her high heels. "Can I help you?"

Cyril saw a small, thin woman in her early forties wearing a nearly transparent white blouse over a tight skirt. She had a small, pinched face and bulging brown eyes. Cyril thought sourly that she looked like a rabbit with myxomatosis. But he gave his most charming smile and said, "I saw that you had books for sale."

"Yes, they're over here," said Hetty, leading the way to a wooden bench. "These are the ones that are too damaged to remain on the shelves. Are you new to the area?"

"Just on holiday," said Cyril. "I'm over in Lochdubh."

"Keep clear of the police station. Hamish Macbeth is useless."

"I'd like to hear more," said Cyril. "I enjoy a bit of gossip with a pretty girl. When do you get off?"

"We close up in ten minutes."

"Let's go for a drink."

"Yes, I would love that," said Hetty.

HETTY HAD NO intention of telling this gorgeous man her real reason for disliking Hamish. She had once invited Hamish to a party at her flat after having met him on one of his investigations. Hamish was not interested. But she had drunk too much and had thrown herself at him, calling him her darling. Hamish had gently pushed her away and gone home. Her friends teased her about it until she began to think Hamish had wronged her. She told them so many times that Hamish had led her on that she began to believe it.

CYRIL WAS OFTEN seen in Hetty's company in the following days. Then, to Hetty's dismay, he said he would be too busy to see her. Hetty began to feel guilty. She was sure Cyril was spying on Hamish and wondered if he was a villain. She had made up a lot of malicious stories about Hamish's laziness. If anything happened to Hamish, the investigation would lead back to her.

She at last phoned Hamish and said someone called Jamie Mackay had been asking a lot of questions about him.

"Don't worry," said Hamish. "I know all about him," correctly guessing that Jamie was Cyril.

"What will you do?" asked Hetty.

"Take my shotgun and blow the bugger's head off," said Hamish and rang off.

"LET'S GIVE CYRIL something to do tomorrow," Hamish said to Dick. "We'll race off tomorrow up north and give the lad something to chase. The beasties are getting fat. They need some exercise."

Hamish's "beasties" consisted of a wild cat called Sonsie and a dog called Towser. "I'll get a picnic ready," said Dick.

Hamish felt a stab of irritation. He wished Dick would not be so—well—*domesticated*. He felt Dick was taking the place of a possible wife, and Hamish often dreamed of marriage. His love affair with television presenter Elspeth Grant had recently fallen through. He had once been engaged to Priscilla Halburton-Smythe, daughter of the retired colonel who owned the Tommel Castle Hotel. But Priscilla's sexual coldness had caused him to break off the engagement.

AT THAT MOMENT, Cyril was ensconced in the Currie sisters' parlour, balancing a cup of tea on one knee. He had hoped the sisters would give him some gossip about Hamish, but they seemed hellbent on quizzing him about the King James Version of the Bible.

"Beautiful words," said Nessie. " 'I am the voice of one crying in the wilderness.' "

"I couldn't agree more," said Cyril, ignoring Jessie's echo. He thought, If I don't get out of this damn place soon I'll go mad. "You were saying something about the local policeman."

"No, I wasn't," said Nessie.

"Bit of a layabout, is he?"

"We do not gossip in this village," said Nessie righteously. "Pass me the Bible, Jessie, and we'll hear this nice young man read to us."

It was a large Victorian Bible, illustrated with steel engravings. Feeling trapped, Cyril began to read, and, as he read, he began to experience a strange feeling of doom. His mobile phone suddenly rang, and he grabbed it out of his pocket. It was Blair, asking if there was any progress.

"Can't talk now, Mother," said Cyril. "I'll call you later." He rang off.

"You shouldn't cut your mother off like that," chided Nessie.

"How right you are." Cyril stood up and put the Bible and his cup on the table. "I'll get back to my digs and call her from there."

"We'll see you in the kirk on Sunday," said Nessie.

If I'm still alive and not dead with boredom, thought Cyril, making his escape.

"WHERE ARE WE off to?" asked Dick the next morning as he climbed into the Land Rover beside Hamish.

"Do you know Sandybeach?"

"No, where's that?"

"Tiny little place up north of Scourie. Grand

place for a picnic. I'll put the siren on and get Cyril chasing us."

"It's only seven in the morning," said Dick. "Think he'll be up yet?"

"Probably not. But I've phoned Jimmy. Blair's bound to ask if there's been a report of a crime, so I told him to say there was a burglary at Sandybeach."

"So what do we do if the scunner catches up with us?"

"He won't. It's so quiet up there, you can hear a car coming for miles. We'll take off for somewhere else."

THE SOUND OF the siren woke Cyril. He tumbled out of bed and dashed to the window, opened it, and hung out. He could just see the Land Rover racing out over the humpbacked bridge. He scrabbled into his clothes and phoned Blair, asking him to find out where Hamish had gone.

He had gone a mile out of Lochdubh when Blair rang. "Burglary at a place called Sandybeach."

"Where's that?"

"How should I know? Look at a map."

Cyril programmed his sat-nav and set off in pursuit. He hurtled along the one-track roads, blind to the beauty all around him. Purple heather blazed on the flanks of the soaring mountains. Rowan trees shone with bloodred berries. Above, the sky was an arch of blue. At one point, he thought he heard the sound of another driver behind him and suddenly stopped, switched off his engine, rolled down the windows, and listened. But there was nothing to be heard but the mournful call of a curlew.

Cyril crouched over the wheel and drove on.

Sutherland, the southland of the Vikings, is the most underpopulated county in the British Isles. The west coast has the most dazzling scenery. But to Cyril, it was an odd foreign landscape, alien, far from the bustle and crowds of Strathbane.

At long last, he saw a signpost pointing the way to Sandybeach.

"The end of the road," said Cyril, not knowing that, for him, it was.

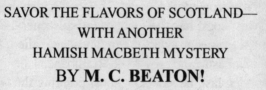

SAVOR THE FLAVORS OF SCOTLAND—
WITH ANOTHER
HAMISH MACBETH MYSTERY
BY **M. C. BEATON!**

*Please turn the page
for a preview of*

Death of Yesterday

Send home my long stray'd eyes to me,
Which O! too long have dwelt on thee

—William Blake

Morag Merrilea was an art student, earning money in her summer holidays by working as a secretary for Shopmark Fashions in Cnothan in the Scottish county of Sutherland. She was English and considered herself a cut above her fellow workers. She was highly unpopular. Her appearance was unprepossessing. She had lank brown hair and rather prominent green eyes. But she had a passion for art and for studying faces.

Shopmark Fashions was a new factory on the outskirts of the village, risen out of an old derelict Victorian furniture store. Cnothan was a grim place with one main street running down to a man-made loch over which towered the grey walls of a hydro-electric dam.

Morag had taken the job because she had dreamt of a romantic highland village, and had never quite got over the culture shock of being in Cnothan where the sour locals took pride in "keeping themselves to themselves."

SHE SAT IN her usual corner of the Highlander pub one Saturday evening with her sketchbook, busily drawing the faces of people in the pub, and, also, the face of someone looking in at the window. Morag always drank alone. The other employees of the factory drank at a pub down on the lochside and, strangely enough, Morag's solitary drinking was not remarked on because of her unpopularity and the locals shying away from any mention of her.

Although not particularly imaginative, she seemed that particular evening to feel the remoteness, the very foreignness of Sutherland pressing in on her, a claustrophobic sense that the great towering mountains were creeping closer across the heathery moors. The result was, she drank more than usual. The pub was quite full with forestry workers, crofters, and the unemployed. Morag was brilliant at drawing faces and felt the very act of drawing people and putting them on paper put them in her power.

At one point, she went to the lavatory. When

she returned, she found her sketchbook was missing. She complained to the barman and to everyone around. Getting nothing in reply but blank stares, she downed her drink and made for the door. Morag collapsed outside and was taken to hospital.

After she came awake the following morning and received a lecture from a young doctor on the evils of drink, Morag was gripped with a sudden fear that she might be an alcoholic. She had drunk four pints of beer and assumed she had experienced a blackout. She could not remember yesterday evening at all.

She did have one friend at Hornsey Art College, where she had studied. She phoned her friend, Celia Hedron, and told her about losing her memory.

Celia said sharply, "Have you considered that someone might have slipped you a date rape drug? That blacks you out so you can't remember things."

This dramatic solution appealed to Morag, who did not like to think she was a common alcoholic. She dithered for a week before catching a bus from Cnothan and presenting herself at the police station in Lochdubh. She had been told that police sergeant, Hamish Macbeth, was also responsible for policing Cnothan—along with vast tracts of Sutherland.

*   *   *

HER FIRST IMPRESSION of Hamish Macbeth was a bad one. When she arrived, he was upon a ladder clearing out the guttering. His lazy constable, Dick Fraser, a plump man with a grey moustache, was sleeping peacefully in the front garden on a deck chair.

"You!" shouted Morag. "Get down here immediately. I have a crime to report."

Hamish came slowly down the ladder. She saw a tall man with flaming red hair and hazel eyes.

"What seems to be the problem?" he asked.

Morag threw back her head and declared, "I have been drugged, raped, and my sketchbook has been stolen."

"Then you'd better come ben to the office," said Hamish mildly.

"Whassat?" mumbled Dick and went back to sleep.

Hamish led the way in at the side door, through the kitchen and into his small office, where he pulled out a chair for her. He wrote down the details of her addresses in Cnothan and London along with her phone numbers at home and work.

"It's like this," said Morag. She gave him her view of what had happened, along with details of her age, twenty-three, and her work as a secretary at the clothes factory.

"And when exactly did this take place?" asked Hamish.

"Last Saturday week."

Hamish had been taking notes. He put down his pen. "If you were drugged with some date rape drug, it would no longer be in your system. Were you checked for signs of rape?"

"Well, no."

"I think we should go to the hospital right away and have you checked."

Morag bit her lip. She had examined herself and knew there were no signs of bruising or forced entry. "I can't be bothered," she said.

"Then I don't see what you expect me to do," said Hamish patiently.

"You are a moron," said Morag. "You could at least make some push to get my sketchbook back—that is if you ever get off your arse and do anything."

"What were you sketching?"

"Faces of people in the pub. Oh, and someone who looked in at the window."

"Are you any good?" asked Hamish bluntly.

She opened her large handbag and pulled out a small sketchpad and handed it to him.

His interest quickened. She was very good indeed.

"I'll need to take a note of who was in the pub. Can you remember any names?"

"They're all just faces to me—Angus this and Jimmy that. I do not consort with the local peasantry. The factory staff drink at the Loaning down on the loch."

"With an attitude like that," said Hamish, the sudden sibilance of his accent showing he was annoyed, "I'm fair astounded that someone didnae try to bump you off instead of chust slipping something in your drink."

"You're as useless as the rest of . . ."

"Calm down, lassie. I hae this idea . . ."

"Wonders will never cease."

"Oh, shut up and listen for once in your life. I know a hypnotist down in Strathbane. He might be able to put you under and restore some o' your memory."

Morag's protruding eyes gleamed. The drama of such a suggestion appealed to her along with the idea of rattling the cage of whoever had drugged her drink.

"I'll make an appointment and let you know," said Hamish.

HAMISH WONDERED AS he set off for Strathbane later that day with Dick why he was even bothering to help such an unlovely character as Morag Merrilea. He cursed himself for not having asked exactly how much she had to drink. She could simply have had an alcoholic blackout.

Still, he reminded himself, he wasn't doing anything else at the moment. The summer was unusually warm with those nasty biting midges of the Highlands out in force. Patel's, the local shop in Lochdubh, had sold out of insect repellent.

As they mounted a crest of the road, Dick said, "Every time I see Strathbane, I'm right glad I'm out of it."

Strathbane was a blot on the beauty of Sutherland. Once a busy fishing port, it had died when the fishing stocks ran out. Drugs arrived, and it became a town with an air of dirt and desolation.

"I don't like this idea of a hypnotist," said Dick. "Sounds awfy like black magic."

"Och, even Strathbane police use Mr. Jeffreys from time to time."

"Did they say they would pay his bill?"

Hamish shifted uncomfortably in the driver's seat. He knew that Detective Chief Inspector Blair, the bane of his life, would have put a stop to it.

"It's fine," he said airily. "He'll just send in his bill as usual."

DICK WAS DISAPPOINTED in Mr. Jeffreys. He had expected to meet an elderly guru.

But Jeffreys was only in his thirties, a thin man with brown hair in a ponytail, dressed in torn jeans and a T-shirt.

"Let me see," said Jeffreys. "I can fit her in at three o'clock next Saturday."

Hamish phoned Morag on her mobile. She was delighted. "Wait till those bastards in the pub hear about this!"

"I wouldnae go around shooting your mouth off," cautioned Hamish. "I'll collect you on Saturday and take you to Strathbane."

IN THE THREE days leading up to Saturday, Hamish and Dick pottered around the police station. To Dick Fraser, a portly man with a grey moustache, it was paradise. Viewed as useless by headquarters in Strathbane, he had been relocated to Lochdubh. He was a quiz addict, appearing on television quiz shows, and the kitchen in the police station gleamed with his winnings—an espresso coffee making machine, a dishwasher, a new washing machine, and a new microwave.

The single and widowed ladies of the village began to regard him as prime husband material, but Dick showed no interest, preferring to dream in a deck chair in the front garden by day and watch television in the evenings.

He was roused from his lethargy on Saturday by Hamish. "We'd better go and pick up yon Morag female," said Hamish. "Get your uniform on."

Morag rented a flat in a Victorian villa on the edge of Cnothan. When Hamish rang her doorbell, there was no reply. Morag's flat was on the top floor. He stood back and looked up. The curtains were open but there was no sign of anyone moving about.

"Silly cow," he muttered. "I'm sure she wouldnae have forgotten." He rang the landlady's bell.

Mrs. Douglas, the landlady, opened the door. She was a small round woman with thick glasses and an untidy thatch of grey hair.

"Whit now?" she demanded.

"We've come to collect Miss Merrilea," said Hamish patiently. "Is herself at home?"

"Dinnae ken."

"Would you please go and look?"

Grumbling, she shuffled off up the stairs. They waited in the warm sunlight.

At last she reappeared and handed Hamish a postcard. "This was stuck on her door," she said.

Typed neatly on a postcard was: "Gone to London. Will be in touch." It was not signed.

"I don't like this," said Hamish. "Would you mind showing us her flat?"

"Have ye a warrant?"

"No, I haff not!" said Hamish. "But if you don't let me in and show me her flat, I'll come back here with a warrant and I will turn this whole damn place upside down, including your premises."

"Here, now, no need for that," she said, thinking of the cash undeclared to the taxman hidden under her mattress. "I'll get the key."

They followed her into a shadowy hall lit with coloured harlequin diamonds of light from the sun shining through the stained-glass panel on the front door.

Dick eyed the steep stairs. "I'll be waiting for ye outside, sir," he said to Hamish.

"Oh, all right," said Hamish crossly.

He followed Mrs. Douglas as she panted up the stairs. She inserted a key into a door on the top landing. "There's no need for you to wait," said Hamish. "I'll bring you down the key when I've finished."

The flat consisted of a small living room, a cell of a bedroom, a kitchen unit behind a curtain, and a shower. The living room contained a small card table laden with artist's materials and two hardback chairs by the window. There was a dingy print of *The Stag at Bay* over the empty fireplace. One battered armchair was beside the fireplace facing a small television set. Planks on bricks along one wall supplied bookshelves.

Hamish went in to the bedroom. He opened the wardrobe. A few skirts and blouses hung there and a winter coat. On top of the wardrobe was a large suitcase. He hauled it down and opened it up. It was empty. He put it back and then opened a chest of drawers. There were various surprisingly saucy items of lingerie: thongs and stockings with lace tops.

He sat down on the bed and looked round. She might have had a backpack of some kind to take a few clothes with her. There was no sign of a handbag, passport, or wallet.

He locked up and went downstairs to where Mrs. Douglas was waiting in the hall. "Did she have a car?" he asked, handing over the keys.

"No, she had a bike."

"And where does she keep it?"

"Just outside. But it's no' there."

"When did you last see her?"

"Cannae bring tae mind."

"Think!"

"Oh, I mind now. It was yesterday morning. Herself was just off tae work."

"Was she carrying a suitcase or any sort of luggage?"

"No. She just got on her bike and went off, same as ever."

Hamish felt uneasy. He put the postcard in a forensic bag and went out to join Dick.

"We'd better check where she works," he said. "I've got a bad feeling about this."

AT SHOPMARK FASHIONS, they found that Morag worked as secretary to the boss, Harry Gilchrist. Mr. Gilchrist kept them waiting ten minutes, which Hamish put down to the usual pompous Scottish boss's way of trying to seem important.

Mr. Gilchrist was a tall thin man in his forties. He had thick black hair in a widow's peak above a sallow face and wet brown eyes.

"Working on Saturday?" asked Hamish.

"Work never stops," said Gilchrist. "What do the police want with me?"

"Did Morag Merrilea turn up for work yesterday?"

"As a matter of fact, she didn't. I meant to send someone to check on her on Monday if she was still absent."

"She left a postcard on the door of her flat saying she had gone to London."

"Isn't that just typical of staff these days!" raged

Gilchrist. "Well, if you come across her, tell her she's fired."

"Did she say anything about going to see a hypnotist?"

"No. A hypnotist? Why?"

Hamish explained about the suspected drugged drink and the missing sketchbook.

"Oh, that? She was complaining about that all over the place. She did drink a fair bit. She was in the habit of making things up."

"Is there anyone she was close to?"

"She kept herself to herself."

Like the whole of bloody Cnothan, thought Hamish.

DICK AND HAMISH next went to the Highlander pub. Pubs all over Britain had been smartened up with restaurants and pleasant décor, but the Highlander had been unmoved by time. There was one dim room with scarred tables and rickety chairs. The walls were still brown with nicotine from the days before the smoking ban. The only food on offer was in a glass case on the counter: tired-looking sandwiches and a solitary mutton pie.

Hamish recognised the barman and owner, Stolly Maguire. Stolly was polishing a glass with a dirty rag when they approached him. He was a thickset man with a bald head with a tank top strained over a beer belly.

Hamish explained they were trying to find out the whereabouts of Morag Merrilea.

"Thon artist?" said Solly. "Havenae seen her. Usually comes in Saturday evening."

"Two Saturdays ago," said Hamish patiently, "did you notice anyone approaching her table when she went to the toilet?"

"Naw. It was fair busy."

Hamish turned round and surveyed the customers, a mixture of crofters, shepherds, builders, and the unemployed.

"Which one of them was here two Saturdays ago?"

"I cannae mind," said Stolly. "Ask them? I saw her collapsing outside the door and phoned for an ambulance."

So Hamish and Dick went from table to table to receive surly answers to the effect that they had seen her on that Saturday but hadn't noticed anyone taking her sketchbook or putting something in her drink.

But a youth with greasy hair said he had noticed a stranger. "Can you describe him?" asked Hamish. "What is your name?"

"Fergus McQueen."

"Well, Fergus, what did he look like?"

"Hard tae tell. He had wan o' thae baseball caps pulled right down. Small and skinny."

"What was he wearing?"

"Black T-shirt, black jeans."

"The cap. Did it have a logo on it?"

"Naw. It was dark green with an orange stripe."

"Give me your address. We may want you to come to Strathbane and help a police artist make a sketch."

BACK AT LOCHDUBH, Hamish sat down at the computer in the police station office and sent over a report. He felt uneasy. It was too much of a coincidence that she should disappear when she had an appointment with the hypnotist.

To his amazement, he got a call from Detective Sergeant Jimmy Anderson later that day. "Blair's decided to look into it," he said.

"Why? I thought he'd delight in shooting the whole thing down," said Hamish.

"I think he feels if there is a crime, then he wants to be the one to solve it. You've stolen his glory too many times."

"I'd better get back to Cnothan and join him."

"He says you're to sit tight and look after your sheep and leave it to the experts."

Hamish groaned. He knew that Blair's blustering,

bullying tactics would make the locals clam up even more.

HAMISH WAITED GLOOMILY for the inevitable. Sure enough, it came later with an e-mail from Blair telling him it was a wild-goose chase and to stop wasting police time and, furthermore, never again try to employ the hypnotist without first getting clearance.

Undeterred, Hamish went back to Cnothan, knocking on doors, questioning one after the other without success.

He was furious when he returned to Lochdubh to receive a phone call from Superintendent Daviot. The locals in Cnothan had complained of police harassment. Blair had found nothing. Hamish was to leave it all alone.

THE WEATHER WAS unusually hot. Three weeks after the disappearance of Morag Merrilea, two men were loading bales of T-shirts onto a lorry outside Shopmark Fashions when they suddenly stopped their work.

"Thon's an awfy smell from that bale," said one, "and it's heavy, too."

"Better cut it open," said his companion. "There's maybe a dead animal inside."

They sliced the twine that held the bale and unrolled it.

The dead and decomposing body of Morag Merrilea rolled out and lay under the eye of the glaring sun.

SAVOR THE FLAVORS OF SCOTLAND—
WITH ANOTHER
HAMISH MACBETH MYSTERY
BY M. C. BEATON!

*Please turn the page
for a preview of*

Death of a Nag

O the disgrace of it!—The scandal,
  the incredible come-down!

—Sir Max Beerbohm

Hamish Macbeth awoke to another day. His dog, Towser, was lying across his feet, snoring rhythmically. Sunlight slanted through the gap in the curtains. The telephone in the police office part of the house shrilled and then the answering machine clicked on. He should rise and go and find out what it was. It was his duty as a police constable of the village of Lochdubh and part of the surrounding area of the county of Sutherland. But all he wanted to do was pull the duvet over his head and go back to sleep.

He could not really think of any good reason for getting up to face the day.

He had, until his demotion from sergeant back to

constable and the end of his engagement with Priscilla Halburton-Smythe, daughter of a local hotelier, been very popular, a happy state of affairs he had taken for granted. But somehow the story had got about that he had cruelly jilted Priscilla, she who had been too good for him in the first place, and so, when he went about his duties, he was met with reproachful looks. Although Chief Superintendent Peter Daviot had also been angry with him over the end of the engagement, that was not why Hamish had been demoted. He had solved a murder mystery by producing what he firmly believed was the body of the murdered man to elicit a shock confession from the guilty party. The ruse had worked, but he had had the wrong body. It had turned out to be a fine example of Pictish man and the police were accused of being clod-hopping morons for having so roughly handled and used such a prime exhibit. Someone had to be punished, and naturally that someone was Hamish Macbeth.

Hamish was not an ambitious man. In fact, he was quite happy with his lot as ordinary police constable, but he felt the displeasure of the village people keenly. His days before his disgrace had pleasantly been given up to mooching around the village and gossiping. Now no one seemed to want to spend the time of the day with him, or that was the way it seemed to his gloomy mind. If Priscilla, whom Hamish considered remarkably unaffected by the end to the romance, had stayed around to demonstrate that fact, then he would not be in bad odour. But she had left to stay with friends in Gloucestershire for an extended visit, so as far as the villagers were concerned, Hamish had driven her off and she was down in "foreign" parts, nursing a broken heart.

Mrs. Halburton-Smythe did not help matters by shaking her head and murmuring "Poor Priscilla" whenever Hamish's name was mentioned, although what Mrs. Halburton-Smythe was sad about was that she was beginning to believe that her cool and aloof daughter did not want to marry anyone.

With a groan, Hamish made the effort and got up. Towser gave a grumbling sound in the back of his throat and slid to the floor and padded off towards the kitchen.

Hamish jerked back the curtains. The police station was on the waterfront and overlooked the sea loch, which lay that morning as calm as a sheet of glass.

He washed and dressed and went through to the police office. The message was from headquarters in Strathbane reminding him he had not sent in a full statement about a break-in at a small hotel on the road to Drum. He ambled into the kitchen and made himself a breakfast of bread and cheese, for he had forgotten to light the stove. Priscilla had presented him with a brand-new electric cooker, but he had childishly sent it back.

He fed Towser and stood on one leg, irresolute, looking like a heron brooding over a pond. Depression was new to him. He had to take action, to do something to lift it. He could start by typing that report. On the other hand, Towser needed a walk.

The phone began to ring again and so he quickly left the police station with Towser at his heels and set out along the waterfront in the hot morning sun. And it was hot, a most unusual state of affairs for the north of Scotland. He pushed his peaked cap back on his fiery-red hair and his hazel eyes saw irritation heading his way in the form of the Currie sisters, Jessie and Nessie.

The eyes of the village spinsters constantly accused him of being a heartless flirt. He touched his cap and said, "Fine morning."

"It is for some. It is for some," said Jessie, who had an irritating habit of repeating things. "Some, on the other hand, are breaking their hearts."

Hamish skirted round them and went on his way. Resentment and self-pity warred in his bosom. He had once helped the Currie sisters out of a dangerous jam and had destroyed evidence to do so. Damn it, he had helped a lot of people in this village. Why should he be made to feel guilty?

His thoughts turned to Angela Brodie, the doctor's wife. Now *she* had not turned against him. He walked up the short path leading to the doctor's house, went round the back and knocked at the kitchen door. Angela answered it, the dogs yapping at her feet. She pushed her fine wispy hair out of her eyes and said vaguely, "Hamish! How nice. Come in and have coffee."

She cleared a space for him at the kitchen table by lifting piles of books off it and placing them on the floor.

"I don't seem to have had a chat with you in ages," said Angela cheerfully. "Heard from Priscilla?"

Hamish, who had just been lowering his bottom onto a kitchen chair, stood up again. "If you are going to start as well..." he began huffily.

"Sit down," said Angela, startled. "Start what?"

Hamish slowly sat down again. "You haff been the only one who hass not gone on about Priscilla," he said, his Highland accent becoming more sibilant, as it always did when he was angry or upset.

"Oh, I see," said Angela, pouring him a mug of coffee and sliding it across the table towards him. "I only asked about Priscilla because I assumed that you and she were still friends."

"And so we are!" said Hamish. "But ye would-nae think so with this lot in Lochdubh. You would think I wass some sort of Victorian philanderer the way they go on."

"It'll blow over," said Angela comfortably. "These sort of ideas spread through these villages like an infection. Mrs. Wellington started it." Mrs. Wellington was the minister's wife. "She started it by complaining that you were a feckless womanizer and things like that. You know how she goes on. But you brought that on yourself!"

"How?"

"She happened to overhear you doing a very good impression of her to delight the Boy Scouts."

"Ah."

"And so she got a resentment to you and shared it around. Resentment is very infectious. It has always fascinated me the way, for example, one malcontent can bring a whole factory out on strike and keep everyone out on strike until the firm folds and they all lose their jobs. Also, you're going around being so gloomy. That fuels it. You look like a guilty man."

"I'm a bit down," confessed Hamish. "The fact is I've taken a scunner tae Lockdubh and everyone in it."

"Hamish! You love the place!"

"Not at the moment."

"You're due some leave, aren't you? Get right away on holiday. You could get one of those cheap holidays in Spain. Or some of the African package holidays are very cheap."

"I'll think about it," said Hamish moodily. "I might just take a wee holiday somewhere in Scotland, seeing that the weather's fine."

Angela got up and began to rummage through a pile of old magazines on a kitchen chair. She extracted a battered Sunday-paper colour supplement. "What about this place?" she said, flipping open the pages. "Skag. Have you been to Skag?"

"That's over on the Moray Firth. I havenae been there, though I've been into Forres, which is quite close." He looked at the coloured photographs. It looked like a Cornish resort with long white beaches, pretty village and harbour. There was also a page of advertisements for hotels and boarding-houses in Skag. "I'll take this with me, Angela, if you don't mind."

"Keep it," said the doctor's wife. "It's one less piece of junk. I can never bring myself to throw magazines out or even take them along to the waiting-room."

"What's the latest gossip?" asked Hamish.

She sipped her coffee and looked at him in that

vague way she always had. Then she put down her coffee-cup and said, "Well, the biggest piece of gossip apart from yourself is Jessie Currie."

"What about her?"

"Angus Macdonald, the seer, told her she would be married before the year's out."

Hamish's hazel eyes lit up with amusement. "She didnae believe him, did she?"

"She says she didn't, but she's been casting a speculative eye over the men of the village and Nessie is worrying about being left alone."

"And who is this charmer who's going to sweep our Jessie off her feet?"

"Angus will only say it's going to be a divorced fisherman."

"We don't have any divorced fishermen!"

"I pointed that out to Jessie and she said, 'Not yet.'"

"Chance'll be a fine thing," said Hamish. "Dried-up old spinster like her."

"Hamish! That's cruel."

"Aye, well, she should mind her own business instead of ither folks'."

"I really do think you need to get away. Willie Lamont was saying the other day that when you go to the restaurant, you're always complaining about something."

Willie Lamont, Hamish's one-time sidekick, had left the police force to marry a young relative of the owner of the Italian restaurant and worked there much harder than he had ever done when he was a police constable.

"The portions are getting smaller and smaller and the prices higher."

"Still, it's not like you to complain. I'll bet if you had a break from all of us, you'd be very happy to come back and see us again."

Hamish got up. "We'll see. Thanks for the coffee."

He walked along the waterfront and perched on the harbour wall. Towser sighed and lay down. Hamish studied the magazine article. There was an advertisement from a boarding-house called The Friendly House "situated right on the beach with commanding sea views, old-fashioned cooking; special low terms for July, halfboard."

Hamish lowered the magazine and looked over at the village. It was a largely Georgian village, built all in the same year by one of the dukes of Sutherland to enlarge the fishing industry, trim little square whitewashed houses facing the sea loch. He knew everyone in the village, from people who had lived there all their lives like the Currie sisters, to the latest incomers. He felt better now he had talked to Angela, much better. He had been seeing things through a distorting glass, imagining everyone was against him.

So when he saw Mrs. Maclean, Archie, the fisherman's wife, stumping along towards him, carrying a heavy shopping basket, he gave her a cheery smile. "Lazing about as usual?" demanded Mrs. Maclean. She was a ferocious housekeeper, never seen without a pinafore and smelling strongly of soap and disinfectant. Her hair was twisted up in foam rollers and covered with a headscarf.

"I am enjoying the day," said Hamish mildly.

"How ye can enjoy anything wi' that poor lassie down in England eating her heart out is beyond me," said Mrs. Maclean.

Hamish studied her thoughtfully and then a gleam of malice came into his eyes. "Priscilla isn't nursing a broken heart, but some poor fisherman's wife is soon going tae be."

"Whit dae ye mean?"

Hamish slid down from the wall, rolled up the colour supplement and put it in his trousers pocket. "Aye, Angus Macdonald told Jessie Currie she'd be married afore the year was out and tae a fisherman, a *divorced* fisherman. How's Archie these days?"

"Archie's jist fine," said Mrs. Maclean, her eyes roving this way and that, as if expecting to see her husband. It was well known in the village that Archie, when not fishing, spent most of the day avoiding his wife, in case she scrubbed him to death, as he put it. "Anyway, it's all havers," she said. "Jessie Currie. The very idea."

And then, to Hamish's delight, he saw Archie in the distance. He came abreast of the Curries' cottage and Jessie called something to him over the garden hedge and he stopped to talk to her.

"There's your man ower there," said Hamish happily, "and talking tae Jessie."

Mrs. Maclean stared in the direction he pointed and gave something that sounded like a yelp and set off at speed. But Archie saw her coming and left Jessie and darted up one of the lanes leading up to the back village and was gone from view.

Hamish strolled back to the police station, phoned Strathbane and said he wanted to take three weeks' immediate holiday. Permission was easily granted. The bane of his life, Detective Chief Inspector Blair, was in Glasgow, there had been virtually no crime at all for months, and so it was agreed that Sergeant Macgregor over at Cnothan could take over Hamish's duties as well as his own. He was free to leave at the end of the week. He phoned the boarding-house in Skag and learned to his delight that, thanks to a cancellation, they had one room free for the very time he wanted, and yes, dogs were allowed.

Feeling happier than he had felt for some time, he then set out to arrange for his sheep to be looked after, his hens and ducks as well, and then decided to pay a visit to the seer to find out what had possessed the old sinner to wind Jessie up like that.

Angus Macdonald, the seer, a big, craggy man like one of the minor prophets, peered all around Hamish looking for a present before he let him in. The villagers usually brought him something, a bottle of whisky or a cake.

"No, I didnae bring you anything," said Hamish, following him into his small living-room. "I don't want your services. I simply want to know what you were doing telling Jessie she was going tae marry a divorced fisherman."

"I seed it," said Angus huffily. "I dinnae make things up."

"Come on, man. Jessie!"

"Well, that's whit I seed."

"That sort o' rubbish could start gossip."

"Maybe that's whit you're hoping fur, Hamish."

"How's that?"

"Stop them gossiping about you and your lassie."

"I think you're an old fraud," said Hamish. "I've always thought you were an old faker."

"You're jist bad-tempered because ye think nobody loves ye. Here's Mrs. Wellington coming."

Hamish jumped up in alarm. He scampered off and ran down the hill, seemingly deaf to the booming hail of the minister's wife.

"That man," said the tweedy Mrs. Wellington as she plumped herself down in an armchair. "I'll be glad to see the back of him."

"Is he going somewhere?" asked Angus.

"I met Mrs. Brodie just before I came up here. She said that Hamish was thinking of going over to Skag for a holiday."

"Oh, aye," said Angus. "Now whit can I dae for you, Mrs. Wellington?"

"This business about Jessie Currie. It can't be true." Her eyes sharpened. "Unless you've heard something."

"I see things," said Angus.

"And you hear more gossip than anyone I know," said Mrs. Wellington sharply. "I brought you one of my fruitcakes. It's over on the counter. You see, Mr. Patel at the stores told me that he had seen Archie Maclean talking to Jessie Currie and when he saw his wife at the other end of the waterfront coming towards him, he ran away."

"I'm saying nothing," said Angus mysteriously. "But we'll jist have a wee cup o' tea and try that cake."

*   *   *

EARLY ON SATURDAY morning, Hamish Macbeth hung a sign on the door of the police station, referring all inquiries to Sergeant Macgregor at Cnothan. He locked the police Land Rover up in the garage, put Towser on the leash, and picked up his suitcase. Then the phone in the police station began to ring. He decided to answer it in the hope that someone in the village might have phoned up to wish him a happy holiday.

The voice of the seer sounded down the line. "I wouldnae go tae Skag if I were you, Hamish."

Hamish felt a superstitious feeling of dread.

"Why not?" he asked.

"I see death. I see death and trouble fur you, Hamish Macbeth."

"I havenae time to listen to your rubbish," said Hamish sharply and put the receiver down.

At the other end of the line, Angus listened to that click and smiled. Called him a fraud, had he? Well, that should give Hamish Macbeth something to think about!

Hamish left the police station and walked along to the end of the harbour to get the bus to Bonar Bridge. From Bonar Bridge he would get another bus to Inverness and then buses from Inverness over to Skag.

The bus was, as usual, late, twenty minutes late,

in fact. Hamish was the only passenger. He often thought the driver, Peter Dunwiddy, deliberately started off late so as to have an excuse to break the speed limit, even with a policeman on board. Hamish hung on tightly and Towser flattened himself on the floor of the bus as it hurtled up out of Lochdubh and then began to scream around the hairpin bends on its way to Bonar Bridge. He expected to feel a lightness of heart as Lochdubh and all its residents fell away behind him. But he felt an odd tugging sadness at his heart. To match his mood, the day was grey, all colour bleached out of the landscape, like a Japanese print. He hoped the good weather would return. Perhaps he should not have been so parochial as to holiday in Scotland. When did Scotland ever guarantee sunny weather and water warm enough to go for a swim?

By the time he reached the village of Skag, he felt as tired as if he had walked there. He asked directions to The Friendly House and then set out. It was about two miles outside the village, and not on the beach exactly but behind a row of sand dunes set a quarter of a mile back from the North Sea.

It was an old Victorian villa, vaguely Swiss-chalet design, with fretted-wood balconies and blue shutters. He glanced at his watch. Half past five. Tea was at six.

He entered a dim hallway furnished with a

side-table holding an assortment of tourist brochures, a large brass bowl holding dusty pampasgrass, a carved chair, and an assortment of wellington boots. He pressed a bell on the wall and a door at the back of the wall opened and a thick, heavy-set man came towards him. He had blond hair and bright-blue eyes and a skin which had a strange high glaze on it, like china. Hamish thought he was probably in his fifties.

"You must be our Mr. Macbeth," he said breezily. "The name's Rogers, Harry Rogers. You'll find us one happy family here. Come upstairs and I'll show you and the doggie your room."

The room boasted none of the modern luxuries like telephone or television. But the bed looked comfortable, and through the window Hamish could see the grey line of the North Sea. "The bathroom's at the end of the corridor," said Mr. Rogers. "As you see, there's a wash-hand basin in the corner there. Tea's at six. Yes, none of this dinner business. Good old-fashioned high tea."

Hamish thanked him and Mr. Rogers left. Towser, tired after the long walk, crawled onto the bed and closed his eyes. Hamish quickly unpacked, taking out a bowl which he filled with water for the dog, and a can of dog food, a can opener, and another bowl. He filled the second bowl with the dog food and put it on the floor beside the water. Spoilt Towser did not like dog food, but, reflected Hamish, he would just need to put up with it for the duration of the holiday. Of course, maybe he could buy him some cold ham as a treat. Towser was partial to cold ham. He changed into a pair of jeans and a checked shirt, debated whether to wear a tie and decided against it, and then went downstairs and pushed open a door marked "Dining-Room." A small, birdlike woman, who turned out to be Mrs. Rogers, hailed him. "Mr. Macbeth, your table's here . . . with Miss Gunnery."

Hamish nodded to Miss Gunnery and sat down. All the other diners were already seated. Mr. Rogers appeared and introduced everyone to everyone else. Hamish's quick policeman's mind noted all the names and his sharp eyes took in the appearance of the other guests.

Miss Gunnery on the other side of the table had the sort of appearance which even in these modern days screamed spinster. She had a severe face, gold-rimmed glasses and a mouth like a trap. Her flat-chested figure was dressed despite the humidity of the day in a green tweed suit worn over a white shirt blouse.

At the next table was a man with his wife, a Mr. and Mrs. Harris. Both were middle-aged. She had neatly permed brown hair and neat, closed features, and was dressed in a woollen sweater and cardigan and a black skirt. Her husband was wearing an open-necked shirt and a trendy black leather jacket and jeans, the sort of outfit that tired businessmen in a search for fading youth have taken to wearing, almost like a uniform. He was grey-haired, had large staring eyes and a bulbous nose.

Beyond them were Mr. and Mrs. Brett and their three children, Heather, Callum, and Fiona, aged seven, four, and three, respectively. Mr. Brett was a comfortable, chubby man with glasses and an air of benign stupidity. His wife was an artificial redhead with a petty face and pencilled eyebrows. Either they were plucked, a rare fashion these days, thought Hamish, or they had fallen off, or she had been born that way. She had pencilled in arches of eyebrows, which gave her a look of perpetual surprise.

At the window table were two girls called Tracey Fink and Cheryl Gamble, both from Glasgow. They both had hair sun-streaked by chemicals rather than sunlight and white pinched faces under a load of make-up, and both were wearing identical outfits, striped black-and-white sweaters and black ski pants with straps under the instep and dirty sneakers. And in a far corner was a solitary man who had the

honour of having a table to himself. His name was
Mr. Andrew Biggar. He had a tanned face and thick
brown hair streaked with grey, small clever brown
eyes, and a long, humorous mouth.

High tea, that famous Scottish meal now hardly
ever served, consists of one main dish, usually cold
ham, and salad and chips, washed down with tea. In
the middle of each table was a cake stand. On the bottom were thin slices of white bread scraped with
butter. On the next layer were scones and teacakes,
and on the top, cakes filled with ersatz cream and
covered in violently coloured icing.

"Grand day," said Hamish conversationally to
Miss Gunnery, for every day in Scotland where it is
not exactly freezing cold and pouring wet is desig-
nated a "grand day."

Her eyes snapped at him through her glasses. "Is
it? I find it damp and overcast."

Hamish relapsed into a crushed silence. He
wished he had not come. But Mr. Harris's voice
rose above the conversation at the other tables, he
of the trendy leather jacket, and caught Hamish's
attention.

"Well, this holiday was your idea, Doris," he
said.

"I only said the tea was a trifle weak," protested
his wife.

"Always finding fault, that's your problem," said Mr. Harris. "If you exercised more and thought less about your stomach, you might be as fit as me."

"I only said—"

"You said. You said," he jeered. He looked around the room. "That's women for you. Always nit-picking."

"Bob, *please*," whispered his wife.

"Please what?"

"*You* know." She cast a scared look around the dining-room. "Everyone's listening."

"Let them listen. I'm not bound by your suburban little fears, my dear." His voice rose to a high falsetto. "What *will* the neighbours think."

And so he went on and on.

The severe Miss Gunnery, who prided herself on "keeping herself to herself," was driven to open her mouth and say to the tall, lanky, red-headed man opposite, "That fellow is a nag."

"Aye, the worst kind," agreed Hamish, and then smiled, and at that smile, Miss Gunnery thawed even more. "Mrs. Harris is right," she said. "The tea is disgustingly weak, the ham is mostly fat, and those cakes look vile. I know this place is cheap..."

"Maybe there's a fish-and-chip shop in the village," said Hamish hopefully. "I might take a walk there later. My dog likes fish and chips."

"Oh, you have a dog? What breed?"

"Towser's a mixture of every kind of breed."

Miss Gunnery looked amused. "Towser! I didn't think anyone called a dog Towser these days—or Rover, for that matter."

"It started as a wee bit o' a joke, that name," said Hamish, "and then the poor animal got stuck wi' it."

"What do you do for a living, Mr. Macbeth?"

The nag's voice had temporarily ceased. There was silence in the dining-room. "I'm a civil servant," said Hamish. He did not like telling people he was a policeman because they usually shrank away from him. And he had found that when he said he was a civil servant, it sounded so boring that no one ever asked him where he worked or in what branch of the organization.

"I'm a schoolteacher," said Miss Gunnery. "I've never been to Skag before. It seemed a good chance to get a cheap holiday."

"When did you arrive?"

"Today, like the rest. We're all the new intake."

Mr. Rogers and his wife hovered about among the tables, snatching away plates as soon as any diner looked as if he or she was finished. "We have television in the lounge across the hall," announced Mr. Rogers. His wife was carefully packing away uneaten cakes into a large plastic box. Hamish guessed, and as it turned out correctly, that they would make their appearance again during the following days until they had all either been eaten or gone stale.

The company moved through to the lounge. Bob Harris had temporarily given up baiting his wife, but Andrew Biggar made the mistake of asking Doris Harris what she would like to see.

"*Coronation Street* is just about to come on," said Doris shyly. "I would like to see that if no one else minds."

Her husband's voice cut across the murmur of assent. "Trust you to inflict your penchant for soaps on everyone else. How you can watch that pap is beyond me."

Hamish walked over to the television set, found "Coronation Street," and turned up the volume. "I like "Coronation Street,'" he lied to Doris. "Always watch it."

He sat down next to Miss Gunnery. He was aware of the nag's voice all through the programme, sneering and jeering at the characters. He sighed and looked about the room. The chairs were arranged in a half-circle in front of the television set. The fireplace was blocked up and a two-bar electric heater stood in front of it. There was a set of bookshelves containing battered paperbacks, no doubt left behind by previous guests. The Rogerses were probably too mean to buy any. The chairs were upholstered in a scratchy fabric. The carpet was a worn-out green with faded yellow flowers. There were various dim pictures on the walls, Highland cattle in Highland mist, and a grim photograph of a Victorian lady who stared down on all. Probably the original owner, thought Hamish.

At the end of the programme, which he had only stayed to watch for Mrs. Harris's sake, he rose and said to Miss Gunnery, "I'm going to walk my dog along to the village and see if there's a fish-and-chips shop. Want to come?"

"I don't eat fish and chips," she said primly, looking down her nose.

The tetchiness that had been in him for months rose to the surface again. "So you prefer that high-class muck we had for tea?"

There was an edge of contempt to his light Highland voice and Miss Gunnery flushed. "I'm being silly," she said, getting to her feet. "I'd enjoy the walk."

Hamish went up to get Towser, but when he descended to the hall again it was to find not only Miss Gunnery waiting for him but the rest of the party, with the exception of the Harrises.

They did not say anything like "We've decided

to come too," but merely fell into line behind the policeman like obedient children being taken for a walk.

Mr. Brett was the first to break the silence. "A stone's throw from the sea," he exclaimed. "You would need to have a strong arm to throw a stone that distance."

"Are ye sure there's a chip shop, Jimmy?" asked Cheryl. She hailed from Glasgow, where everyone was called Jimmy, or so it seemed, if you listened to the inhabitants.

"I don't know," said Hamish. "May be something in the pub."

"I'm starving," confided Tracey, stooping to pat Towser. "I could eat a horse between two bread vans."

Cheryl slapped her playfully on the back and both girls giggled.

"It's a pity little Mrs. Harris couldn't come as well," said Andrew Biggar. "Don't suppose she gets much fun. Are you in the army, by any chance, Mr. Macbeth?"

"Hamish. I'm called Hamish. No, Andrew. Civil servant. What makes ye say that?"

"When I first saw you, I thought you were probably usually in uniform. Got it wrong. I'm an army man myself. Forcibly retired."

"Oh, those dreadful redundancies," said Miss Gunnery sympathetically. "And us so soon to be at war with Russia again."

"Don't say that," said Mrs. Brett, whose name turned out to be June, and her husband's, Dermott. "It's been a grim enough start. That man Harris should be shot."

"You can say that again," said Dermott Brett, so June predictably did and the couple roared with laughter at their own killing wit.

"I don't know if I'm going to be able to bear this holiday," murmured Miss Gunnery to Hamish.

"Och," said Hamish, who was beginning to feel better, "I think they're a nice enough bunch of people and there's nothing like a common resentment for banding people together." He winced remembering how common resentment had turned the villagers of Lochdubh against him.

"Harris, you mean," said Miss Gunnery. "But his voice does go on and on and it's not a very big place."

They arrived at the village of Skag. It consisted of rows of stone houses, some of them thatched, built on a point. The river Skag ran on one side of the point and on the other side was the broad expanse of the North Sea. The main street was cobbled but the little side streets were not surfaced and the prevalent white sand blew everywhere, dancing in little eddies on a rising breeze. "Getting fresher," said Hamish. "Look there. A bit of blue sky."

They walked down to the harbour and stood at the edge. The tide was coming in and the water sucked greedily at the wooden piles underneath them. Great bunches of seaweed rose and fell. Above them, the grey canopy rolled back until bright sunlight blazed down.

Hamish sniffed the air. "I smell fish and chips," he said, "coming from over there."

They set out after him and found a small fish-and-chips shop. Hamish suggested they walk to the beach and eat their fish and chips there.

They made their way with their packets past the other side of the harbour, where yachts were moored in a small basin, the rising wind humming and thrumming in the shrouds. There was a sleazy café overlooking the yacht basin, still open but empty of customers, the lights of a fruit machine winking in the gloom inside.

A path led round the back of the café, past rusting abandoned cars and fridges, old sofas and broken tables, to a rise of shingle and then down to where the shingle ended and the long white beach began.

"You spoil that dog," said Miss Gunnery as Hamish placed a fish supper on its cardboard tray down in front of Towser.

Hamish did not reply. He knew he spoilt Towser but did not like anyone to comment on the fact.

"Why does a woman like Doris marry a pillock like that?" asked Andrew Biggar.

June Brett nudged her chubby husband playfully in the ribs. "They're all saints before you marry them and then the beast comes out."

Dermott Brett snarled at her and his wife shrieked with delight. Faces could be misleading, thought Hamish. June looked rather petty and mean when she was not speaking, but when she did, she became transformed into a good-natured woman. The Brett children were making sandcastles down by the water. They were remarkably well behaved. Heather, the seven-year-old, was looking after her young brother and toddling sister, making sure the little Fiona did not wander into the water. Long ribbons of white sand snaked along the harder damp surface of the sand underneath and then there came a haunting humming sound.

"Whit's that?" cried Cheryl, clutching Tracey.

"Singing sands," said Hamish. "I remember hearing there were singing sands here but I forgot about it."

"It's eerie," said Miss Gunnery. "In fact, the whole place is a bit odd. It never gets dark this time of year, does it, Hamish?"

He shook his head, thinking that the place was

indeed eerie. Because of the bank of shingle behind the beach and the flatness of the land behind, there was a feeling of being cut off from the rest of the world. He remembered the seer's prediction with a shudder and then his common sense took over. Angus had heard the gossip about his holiday and had invented death and trouble to pay Hamish back for having called him a fraud.

Miss Gunnery was carefully collecting everyone's fish-and-chip papers when Hamish heard Dermott Brett say, "He's got worse."

"Who?" asked Andrew, lazily scraping in the sand for shells.

"Bob Harris."

"You know him?" asked Hamish.

"Yes, he was here last year."

Miss Gunnery paused in her paper-gathering. "You mean you stayed here and *came back!*"

"New management," said Dermott Brett. "It was owned by a couple of old biddies. They did a good tea, but their prices were quite high for a boarding-house. We weren't going to come back, because with the three kids it was coming to quite a bit. Then June saw the ad with the new cheap prices, but it said nothing about new management."

"What happened to the old women who owned it?" asked Hamish, ever curious.

"They were the Blane sisters, the Misses Blane. Rogers said they took a small house for themselves in Skag. Might call on them, if I can find them."

"So Harris is worse now?" pursued Hamish.

"He was bad enough last year, but in fits and starts. Didn't go on like he does now the whole time. Maybe he'll have settled down by tomorrow. Doris Harris wanted to come with us, but he ranted on at her when you were upstairs getting your dog about wasting good money on fish and chips when she had already eaten."

There was a scream of delight from the Brett children. Heather had placed the three-year-old Fiona on Towser's back. Towser was standing patiently, looking puzzled, his eyes rolling in Hamish's direction for help.

"Leave him be," shouted Hamish. Heather obediently lifted Fiona off Towser's back and Towser lolloped up the beach and lay panting at Hamish's feet.

"Time I got those kids in bed," said June. "They've been on the train all day."

"Come far?" asked Hamish.

"From London."

Dermott got to his feet and brushed sand from his trousers. He walked up to the children and swung the toddler onto his shoulders. June joined him, and the family set off together in the direction of the boarding-house.

"That's a nice family," said Miss Gunnery, returning from a rubbish bin on the other side of the shingle, where she had put the papers. "Perhaps we should be getting back as well."

"Whit aboot the night-life o' Skag?" sniggered Cheryl. "Me and Tracey'd like a drink."

"How old are you?" demanded Miss Gunnery severely.

Cheryl tossed her long blonde hair. "Old enough," she said. Her heavily made-up eyes flirted at Hamish. "Aye, old enough fur anything, isn't that right, Tracey?"

"Sure is," said Tracey in a dreadful imitation American accent. "So let's just mosey along to the pub."

"Bound to be bottled beer up here," said Andrew, "but I'm willing to try it. What about you, Hamish?"

"As long as they'll let Towser in."

"He's married tae his dug!" shrieked Cheryl.

Hamish's thin, sensitive face flushed angrily. He was ashamed of his affection for his dog, ashamed sometimes of Towser's yellowish mongrel appearance.

"I think a drink's just what we all need," said Andrew quickly. "Come along, Hamish."

Hamish had a sudden desire to sulk. But Miss Gunnery said, "I saw the pub near the harbour. It looked quite pretty. I think I'll go after all." She linked a bony arm in Hamish's as he stood up and the small party set off.

It was a pretty thatched pub with tubs of flowers at the door, more like an English inn than a Scottish one. But inside it was as plastic and dreary as the worst of Scottish pubs. A juke-box blared in the corner and a spotty moron was operating the fruit machine with monotonous regularity, his mouth hanging open as he fed in the coins. Hamish had noticed a table and chairs outside and suggested they take their drinks there. Cheryl and Tracey had rums and Coke, Miss Gunnery, a gin and tonic, Andrew, a bottle of beer, and Hamish, a whisky and a bag of potato crisps for Towser.

"There's a carnival here tomorrow," said Hamish. "Sideshows and everything. I saw a poster about it on the pub wall."

"I didn't see a fairground," said Andrew.

"It'll be here tomorrow all right," said Hamish, wise in the ways of Highland gypsies. "They come in the night like a medieval army and the next day, there they all are."

They finished their drinks and walked slowly back to the boarding-house. Cheryl and Tracey had decided to compete for the attention of Hamish Macbeth and so they walked arm in arm with him while Miss Gunnery and Andrew followed behind.

When they went into the boarding-house, Hamish collected a couple of paperbacks from the book-shelves in the lounge and went up the stairs to his room.

It was then that he found out that the Harrises had the room next door. Bob Harris's voice rose and fell, going on and on and on, punctuated by an occasional whimper from his wife.

Hamish wondered whether to go next door and tell the man to shut up, but as a policeman he had found out the folly of interfering in marital prob-lems. Doris would probably round on him and tell him to leave her husband alone.

Or rather, that's what the lazy Hamish Macbeth told himself.

VISIT US ONLINE AT

WWW.HACHETTEBOOKGROUP.COM

FEATURES:

OPENBOOK BROWSE AND
SEARCH EXCERPTS
•
AUDIOBOOK EXCERPTS AND PODCASTS
•
AUTHOR ARTICLES AND INTERVIEWS
•
BESTSELLER AND PUBLISHING
GROUP NEWS
•
SIGN UP FOR E-NEWSLETTERS
•
AUTHOR APPEARANCES AND TOUR
INFORMATION
•
SOCIAL MEDIA FEEDS AND WIDGETS
•
DOWNLOAD FREE APPS

BOOKMARK HACHETTE BOOK GROUP
@ WWW.HACHETTEBOOKGROUP.COM